KATE ROBERTS
Feet in Chains

Translated from the Welsh
by John Idris Jones

seren

Seren is the book imprint of
Poetry Wales Press Ltd
Nolton Street, Bridgend, Wales
www.seren-books.com

Original Welsh, *Traed Mewn Cyffion* © Kate Roberts, 1936
This translation © John Idris Jones, 1977

ISBN 1-85411-321-6

A CIP record for this title is available from
the British Library

Cover painting: study for
Autumn Day with Blue Sky, The Nant Ffrancon Valley
by Peter Prendergast.

*The publisher works with the financial assistance of the
Arts Council of Wales*

Printed in Plantin by CPD (Wales), Ebbw Vale

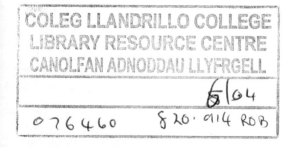

...thou destroyest the hope of man. Thou prevailest forever against him, and he passeth: thou changest his countenance, and sendest him away. His sons come to honour, and he knoweth it not; and they are brought low, but he perceiveth it not of them.

Book of Job 14.20, 21

CHAPTER ONE

The hum of insects, gorse crackling, the murmur of heat, and the velvet tones of the preacher endlessly flowing. Were it not in the open air, most of the congregation would have been asleep. It was a Sunday in June and the Methodists of Moel Arian were holding their preaching festival in the open because the chapel could not hold this many people. It was the year 1880.

The preacher was carried forward by the flood-tide of his eloquence. Everything was to his advantage: the large congregation before him; a warm, quiet day; the wide, blue sky; the distant sea, and the range of mountains behind him. People and nature were spellbound before him and he was able to preach effortlessly, restricted only by his clothes and collar pressing in on him.

His pulpit was a cart with its shafts raised. He was an impressive figure. There was something fascinating in his face. His Roman nose stood out over his cleanshaven upper lip. He had gentle blue eyes, red wavy hair and long side-whiskers. The eyes of those in the front of the crowd were riveted on him but there was a restlessness on the fringes, especially among the young women. Their new shoes were pinching, their stays were too tight and the high collars of their new frocks were almost choking them. They wiped the perspiration from their brows and shuffled their feet.

One of these was Jane Gruffydd, who had recently married Ifan, the son of y Fawnog. Her waist was one of the narrowest, the result of hard pulling on the laces of her stays before leaving for the meeting. Her bustle was the biggest, the satin of her dress the stiffest and heaviest, her frock had the most frills and her hat carried the biggest feather. Many

7

eyes were turned on her because few women owned a dress that could stand up on its own. The best they could afford was French merino. They could not afford a gold chain to hang on a button on the bodice. But there was a greater curiosity because Ifan y Fawnog had been all the way to the Lleyn peninsula in search of a wife. She was tall, and wore her clothes well. Apart from her hair – which today she wore low on her neck – she was not pretty, but there was strength in her face. Jane knew that she was attracting attention and she prayed for the sermon to end. Beads of sweat were gathering in her armpits and she thought of the damage being done to her dress, but the preacher went on and on, his voice rising and falling like that of a man possessed.

Jane was not accustomed to a long sermon because before her marriage she had attended church, not chapel. If the preacher did not stop soon she would faint, and the young women in the congregation would draw their own conclusions about that, and perhaps they would not be far wrong. At last, the sermon ended. The final hymn was being sung and she managed to tell Ifan to invite his friends home to tea while she hastened away to put the kettle on. She quickly picked her way across the farmyard, pulling the braid around her waist and so lifting the hem of her skirt. When she reached the house she undressed and lay on the bed, wallowing in the cool freedom. She then rose and put on her working stays, bodice and skirt and a white apron. She had fortunately begun to prepare tea before leaving for the meeting.

Around her table were people who had come from far for the preaching festival. Jane was happy: the house shone, including the old dresser and clock which her mother had given her, the old oak chairs, and the food was good. She was glad she had sufficient of the new-fashioned little plates to hold cake and jam. She stole glances at Ifan: he did not seem to be completely at ease. A short time before he had been enjoying the sermon, in his black waistcoat and

8

pinstripe trousers. But now he seemed in a bad humour and frowned each time a young woman named Doli spoke. Jane did not know any of the people present but she did her best to be hospitable because they had been invited by Ifan. Something must be troubling him or he would not be so quiet. Perhaps he was annoyed with her for leaving before the end of the meeting: well, there it was, what was done was done. This Doli spoke more than anybody, and while waiting for her tea she looked closely around the kitchen and when Jane rose to fill the teapot Doli's eyes scrutinised the lines of her body. When she said something complimentary a half-mocking smile would appear at the corner of her mouth. She said about the plates, "You certainly do live in style here." And afterwards in the bedroom when she was putting her hat on before going to the evening meeting, "Dear me, you do have a grand place – washstand, dressing-table and all."

"My mother gave them to me," replied Jane. They were made of mahogany and the washstand had a white marble top.

As had been arranged earlier, Jane did not go to chapel that evening, and as Ifan left with the visitors, he gave his wife a half-pleading, half-apologetic look. She thought how handsome he was in his wedding suit.

The cows plodded their way into the cowshed. They impatiently licked at the coarse bran and Indian corn as Jane tied the chains around their necks. After they had finished eating, they slept on their feet. Jane sat on a stool, looking in the direction of the sea, her head resting on a cow's flank. Everything seemed so peaceful. Yet she was not content. She thought of when they were having tea. Something was wrong. Then she thought of the working clothes to be washed the next morning, which was unaccustomed work for her.

She took the cows back to the field. They would hardly put one foot in front of the other. She tried to hurry them by placing one hand on the last one's rump and pushing. The sun was sinking into the sea behind them and their shadows were thrown a long way ahead, making the cows appear as if they would be going on forever. One of them was near to calving. The sound of the spring flowing into the pond was hard and clear. There was no sign of life anywhere apart from an occasional man out for a stroll with a baby in a shawl while his wife was at chapel, or a sick man sitting by his door.

Ifan came back early: he had run home before the fellowship meeting. Before Jane could say anything he blurted out,

"Will you ever be able to forgive me, Jane?"

"What on earth for?"

"Because that Doli came to tea."

"Why, wasn't she supposed to come?"

"No," he struck the arm of his chair with his fist. "She wormed her way here in the company of Bob Owen. People think they can do such things when there is a preaching festival. I never asked her. The shameless hussy. Ah, that I should say such a thing after such a good sermon."

"Well, for sure, I myself did not take to her. She kept praising things too much in a spiteful sort of way."

Ifan explained that this was Doli Rhyd Garreg, whom he once went out with and was going to marry. But when his father was killed in the quarry and the responsibilities of looking after the family fell on him because he was the oldest unmarried son, he had to put off getting married. Doli got tired of waiting and began to flirt with other boys. That finished him.

"Now I can see why she wanted to come here for tea," said his wife. "I'm so glad I put the best things on the table."

10

CHAPTER TWO

The Monday after the preaching festival, Sioned Gruffydd – Ifan's mother – thought it prudent to visit her daughter-in-law in Ffridd Felen. Having her daughter Geini to wash for her, she did not care how inconvenient her presence would be in anybody else's house on a washday: she would have to visit her sometime, and as far as she was concerned Monday was as good a day as any. She would not have much in common with Jane but the previous day's preaching festival would provide a topic of conversation.

At the time, Jane was busy scouring the quarryman's clothes on an old table outside by the spring. She was scrubbing the corduroy trousers after the first washing; the water squeezed out was thick and grey. With the back of the hand holding the brush she wiped the sweat off her face and pushed back a lock of hair. The working-jacket was boiling on the fire in the house.

She heard a shout from the direction of the house, and went there. Her heart sank when she saw it was her mother-in-law. She dreaded breaking the ice, and it would be worse on a day when she wanted so much to get on with her work.

"Don't give up," said Sioned Gruffydd. "I'll set myself down here for a moment," and she lowered herself down on a stone by the spring.

Jane did not want to carry on with this unaccustomed work before the critical gaze of her mother-in-law.

"No, let's go into the house," said Jane. "I was going to have a cup of tea after putting these trousers on the boil."

Taking the trousers from the table and rinsing them in a bucket of clean water from the spring, she carried them into the house.

"Washing working-clothes is a tiring old job," said Sioned.

"Yes, but I'll get used to it," said Jane.

"I don't know. You mark my words, washing a quarry-man's clothes will be something you'll never get used to."

"Well, when I was eight I knew nothing of work, but when I was eighteen I was quite capable. I'll get used to this."

And there'll be more clothes to wash as you get older," said her mother-in-law.

"And perhaps there will be daughters to help me," said the daughter.

Jane was doing her best to hold her tongue, but she saw little that was likeable in her mother-in-law.

Placing the trousers in the big pan, Jane pulled it to one side of the fire and put the kettle in its place. She had nothing but bread and butter and cheese to offer her visitor.

"How did you like the sermon yesterday?" asked Sioned, going off on another tack.

"All right, I suppose, except it was much too long for a hot afternoon," was Jane's reply.

"Well, certainly, for someone with such a narrow waist it must have been very trying to stand all that time."

"It seemed to me that the men were just as tired as the women."

"I suppose you have not been used to long sermons in Church."

"No, but we are quite used to standing for a long time."

"Where do you think you'll be going – the Church or the Chapel?"

"It depends on whether I'll like the Church here. It's far; but if I like it I won't mind the distance."

"I don't think Ifan will like you going to Church."

"Ifan and I talked about things like that before we were married, and he doesn't mind where I go."

"His father would have been surprised to hear Ifan say such a thing."

"So his father was a staunch chapel-goer?"

"Yes, of course. He was one of the first to want a Chapel built here. He would think it very strange that one of his family would pass the Chapel to go to Church."

"What a blessing it is that the dead can't think at all."

Sioned Gruffydd affected a shudder at hearing such blasphemy.

"I heard that you had many here for tea yesterday."

"Yes."

"Geini thought she would be invited."

"Well, why didn't she come then? She would have been very welcome. I came from the meeting a little time before the others and I left it to Ifan to ask whom he liked."

"Doli Rhyd Garreg was here, wasn't she?"

"Yes, she was the one who came uninvited."

"I expect she feels she has some claim on Ifan."

"Ifan certainly didn't want to see her."

"He shouldn't be like that. Doli's a fine young woman."

Jane flushed with anger. She blurted, "Yes, she was certainly good to you, that you were able to keep Ifan for so long."

"That was lucky for you," her mother-in-law replied."

"I won't deny that, and you can't deny that it was even more lucky for you."

"Oh, I don't know. Perhaps it would have been better for Ifan if he had married when he was younger."

The reply was sharp: "It would have been better perhaps for Doli or someone else, but not for you or me."

"Doli would have made him a good wife."

"And Ifan would have made her a good husband, but he made you a better son." Jane said this in a perfectly self-possessed manner, and Sioned Gruffydd was silenced.

After she had gone, Jane was angry with herself for having answered her mother-in-law in such biting terms on her first visit, but she consoled herself with the thought that she had been provoked. She was afraid that Ifan would be hurt by it.

She replaced the washing-pan on the fire, and started to clean the kitchen as the clothes boiled. She then took them back to the spring, where she heard someone call, "Hullo." It was Geini, Ifan's sister, and Jane trembled.

"Don't be afraid," said Geini. "You'll be fed up with seeing our family today. I ran down in case Mother had been nasty to you."

"I'm afraid I was the one to be nasty," said Jane.

"About time someone put her in her place. But let me see, I'll finish washing these for you. Lend me your sack-apron."

After snatching the scrubbing-brush she set to work on the clothes with her strong arms which had been bared to the elbows already.

"I'll run to the house then," said Jane, "and make a pancake or two for tea."

Within half-an-hour Jane called Geini to tea, and found her pegging out the clothes on the line in the field.

"You mustn't pay any attention to Mother," said Geini. "I can guess what she said to you this morning. She's not angry with you, but with Ifan for having married at all. You see, mother is the sort of woman who needs a man to look after her all the time, and when my father was killed he filled the gap only too well."

"It was a pity he married at all then," said Jane.

"Certainly not," replied Geini. "Mother had Ifan long enough to save money at his expense, and all the other children were allowed to go their own way without raising a hand to help. It will do mother a world of good to have to fend for herself."

"What made me mad was to hear her praising that Doli."

"Mother praising Doli!" Geini laughed. "I never heard such a thing! She never had a good word for her until she married that Little Steward. But don't worry about mother: judging by how she was this morning, you've done the best possible thing for her. She's seen that she's met her match. She'll leave you alone now. Anyway, these pancakes are lovely."

"There are plenty of them. I put some cream from the top of the milk on them." Steeped in butter, the pancakes slipped from the fork on to Geini's plate.

"Look," said Geini as she was leaving, "We'll have to visit grandmother one of these days. I'm sure you 'll like her."

CHAPTER THREE

It was a hot day at the end of June and Jane and Geini were crossing Waun Goch towards Allt Eilian to visit Geini's grandmother. They picked their way along sheep-tracks between gorse and heather. Sometimes the hems of their long skirts would catch at a sprig of gorse and as they raised their skirts the gorse scratched their legs. The heat danced before their eyes like gnats. They could hear the sound of slates sliding down from the quarry tip, and far away the sound of firing at the Llanberis quarry. An expanse of countryside lay before them, and to their left was the sea.

Jane frequently looked back in the direction of the Eifl, and felt *hiraeth* as she thought of her home beyond those mountains. This land here was alien to her. She was not used to the sound of shot-firing or the sight of heaps of rubble. There beyond the Eifl there were expensive farms. The houses might appear cold and inhospitable, but to those who knew them they were warm and friendly. And here she was – Jane Sarn Goch – in the midst of strangers in a land where houses, though more frequent, were less friendly to her. What were her father and mother doing now, she wondered. Having tea, probably.

"Are you still homesick?" said Geini, seeing her turn for the fifth time.

"Now and again," she answered. "I've only a wish for a quick visit. It'll get better in time."

"We'll have a good time with Nain, she's from Lleyn." Jane felt better hearing this.

When they got there, Nain – Betsan Gruffydd – was sitting by the fire in that expectant attitude of old people, an attitude of expecting nothing. Geini went straight in, calling,

"Is there anybody at home?"

"Who's there?" came a voice from the corner.

The old lady put her hand up to shield her eyes from the sunlight streaming through the window.

"Oh, it's you Geini. And who is this strange girl with you?"

"Jane, Ifan's wife, come to visit you."

"How are you, my girl?" said the old lady, offering her hand. "Sit down," and she gave up her chair with the semi-circular seat, to Jane.

The old woman wore a woollen petticoat with a loose bodice over it and a blue and white apron. On her head was a white cap with a lace frill. The cap was tied under her chin and over it she wore a small round black hat. Her stringy throat showed between the capstrings and her shawl. In the room was dark oak furniture – a dresser, clock, two-piece cupboard. A brass pan was hanging from the side of the dresser that was full of old-fashioned china. On the walls hung family portraits of many generations.

"Geini," said the old lady, "Put some water in this kettle here." Then she put some more dried cow-dung on the fire and poked it until a flame broke through.

"Do you think you'll like it in these parts?"

"Yes," replied Jane. "It is strange at first, that's all."

"It will be all right when you have children; your roots will have caught by then."

She turned to Geini who had just come in with the kettle, "Make some tea for us, that's a good girl. Do you know, I've gone so that I don't want any food because it's too much of a bother to prepare it. And would you," she addressed Geini again, "look in the hens' nests for some eggs. The people of Lleyn like eggs: I used to have two eggs when I went out to tea."

Jane laughed, beginning to feel at home.

"But I remember little of my time there. I was only four

when I came here, but when I was a young girl I went back there once. I was a maidservant on a large farm at the lower end of this parish, but I found the work too heavy. I gave up my place before getting another. There was no room for me to sleep at home, so I went to my grandmother's in Lleyn. I walked all the way. But," said the old lady, conspiratorially, putting her hand on Jane's knee, "how are things between you and Sioned? Has she been to see you yet?"

"Yes, last Monday morning."

"Was she nice to you?"

"Well, no. I'm afraid I answered her back rather sharply."

"You can't stand up for yourself too much where Sioned is concerned, I'll be bound."

And, leaning towards Jane until her head was almost in the chimney, she whispered, "Sioned is an old shrew. That I should say such a thing about my daughter-in-law! William had to put up with a lot from her, and she did not spare a sigh for him when he died – the poor man. He came to a strange end."

"He was killed, wasn't he?"

"Yes, when he was leaving work one night. He was gathering his things together and was just starting to climb the ladder when there came a great fall of rubble. But Sioned took it in her stride. Ifan was a son to her and a father to the children, even though most of them were old enough to fend for themselves. The more you do for people, the more they expect you to do. Don't be too willing to begin with, my girl. You hold your ground if Sioned tries to get you under her thumb."

Geini came into the house, "Your old hens are not very good at laying, Nain."

"How many have you got?"

"Four."

"Oh, that'll do. Boil a couple each for you two and one for me. There's one in the bowl on the dresser."

"Yes, I was telling you," she went on, "that I had been staying with my grandmother in Mynydd y Rhiw. I never knew kinder people in my life. Granny and I were invited out to tea nearly every day, and we had eggs – always two – or a salted herring boiled with potatoes in their jackets, or a salted flatfish, fried. At that time there wasn't a house there worth calling a house: a house was only four walls and a thatched roof. There was a peat fire on the floor and two wooden beds. When someone died in the house you had to sleep in the same place as the coffin. Dear me, things have changed. Nowadays, every house has two lovely rooms."

The three then enjoyed their meal on the round well-scrubbed table.

As she walked home over the mountain Jane could not help but smile, thinking of the old woman craftily getting Geini out of the way so that she could criticise her daughter-in-law. It is obvious that people's behaviour is the same in every age. She felt closer to the old lady than to any of her husband's family except Geini. Strange what little things brought people together in strong ties of friendship.

CHAPTER FOUR

Elin, the elder baby, sat on the table, stiff as a poker, having been firmly warned not to move. For the time being she had no desire to disobey for the weather was hot and the ribbon of her bonnet was scratching her chin. In the rocking-chair, her mother struggled to get a frock over the head of the younger baby, Sioned, who refused to put her arm into the sleeve. She pushed her fist into her mouth and dribbled down her clean frock.

Then the mother took the two babies to the pram outside the door and placed them side-by-side on the long seat. Strapping them tightly so that the younger would not fall out, she pulled the oilcloth up over their legs. Sometimes she wondered if taking the babies out for a morning walk was worth the trouble of hurrying the morning's housework. Occasionally she would knead the dough the night before and light a fire under the oven at five in the morning just to go out with the children. She was almost exhausted before starting. But there was always the hope of keeping the children quiet and the chance of a chat with someone on the way.

With two cows and a calf, two pigs and two babies, one two-and-a-quarter years and the other six months, she had no time to go visiting even if she wanted to. She could not go to someone's house for 'elevenses' like those women who lived in town houses. But perhaps it was just as well, because she wouldn't be able to follow the talk about local people and events from the past. She did enjoy taking the children out like this, enjoyed dressing them in their red, ribbed dresses, their white petticoats with embroidered hems and starched bonnets. She felt that life was good. Up to now she had wanted for nothing. The money from the pigs came to pay the rates and the interest on the money they borrowed to buy the smallholding. Sometimes they managed to pay back some of the capital from the wages. One day they would repay it all and the property would be theirs.

These were Jane Gruffydd's thoughts as she pushed the pram in the direction of the mountain. Sometimes she would feel it a pity that the two children in front of her were not boys – they would bring more money into the house than girls. But, really, Elin and Sioned were very pretty little things. To her, looking at them from behind, they were delightful, the peaks of their bonnets standing up stiffly and Sioned's curls peeping through the holes in the embroidery. She would lean forward on the strap. Elin would sit up straight, giving Sioned an occasional slap.

They came to the cart-track leading to the mountain, the same mountain that they crossed to see Ifan's grandmother. The road was narrow and hard on the feet. There was heather and gorse, dank moss and peat bogs. The gorse was small and pliable, its flowers of the palest primrose yellow: the short heather made a contrast to it and the dark land around them. Little rivulets ran from the mountain down to the road and then flowed on, sparkling, to the gravelly parts on the sides. Sometimes a stream would run into a pool and stay there. Sheep-tracks everywhere criss-crossed the mountain and all over it sheep and mountain-ponies grazed. Everything associated with the mountain seemed stunted – the gorse, the moss, the sheep, the ponies. The silence would be broken by the cry of the lapwing as it skimmed through the air, suddenly to land on the mountain and run towards its nest in a hole – the hoof-mark of a horse, perhaps.

Jane rested, taking the children from the pram and sitting them on a shawl on the mountain, while she sat day-dreaming. Her thoughts were of her own life. She would not have time except on a lazy May afternoon like this to wonder whether she was happy or not; such a question would hardly ever occur to her. She had been very happy during her courting days, but she had the sense to know that life would not go on at such a pitch of emotion. Ifan was everything she had hoped for but he was much more tired-looking now than when she saw him the first time he came to Lleyn with Guto the Drover. In her own mind she knew well that working in the quarry and running the small-holding was too much for him. But what was to be done? She had heard enough about the quarries to know how uncertain were the wages; and it was a wonderful thing to have plenty of milk and butter. One thing troubled her greatly – that was the condition of the house. The kitchen was the only comfortable room. The bedrooms, especially the back one, were damp and quite unhealthy for anyone to sleep in. The dampness ran down the walls, spoiling the paper, and water dripped on to the bed from the wooden ceiling during frosty weather. She would like to have a new part built alongside the old house so that she would at least have a good parlour and two bedrooms. There were enough stones on Ffridd Felen to build such an extension, and getting rid of the stones would improve the land. But Ifan would have to blast the stones and that would be more work for him. So what was the use of day-dreaming?

She looked across at the village nestling in the warmth of the afternoon. Up there on the left was the quarry with its rubble-heap winding its way down the mountainside. From afar, the slate rubble looked black and reflected the rays of the sun. This was the quarry where Ifan's father had been killed. Who emptied the first tram ever under that huge heap? Whoever it was, he must be dead and buried by now. And who would be the last one to throw his load of rubble from its top? What was she, Jane Gruffydd from Lleyn, doing in this place? But after all it was no worse for her here than in Lleyn. She had to be somewhere. And what was the point of dreaming like this?

The sad cry of a lamb came from afar, and the cackle of geese from a nearby farm. There was something sad in the whole landscape, the quarry, the village and the mountain that seemed tied to one another.

But the next moment Jane was happy, she and her children, happier perhaps than she would be again for a long time.

CHAPTER FIVE

Ifan was very ill with pneumonia and Jane felt that she was to blame for it. She had not been able to resist telling him about her plans for the house extension, and the idea took hold of him. He could not rest until he had gathered enough stones from his land. Every evening and Saturday afternoon the sound of his hammer and chisel was heard through the district, followed by the sharp crack of the explosion. And now illness had overtaken him before the house was ready, the result of the hard work. After a few years of uneventful and trouble-free life, Jane now found herself in a storm in which every minute seemed as long as every year of her married life. She felt as if she had never lived before. How bitterly she regretted ever having mentioned to her husband the dampness of the bedrooms! How on earth was she going to pay the extra interest on the money borrowed to build the new part if Ifan died? That was what troubled her, even though her conscience said she should only be worrying about the possibility of Ifan's death.

During the nine days that Ifan hung between life and death, Jane saw more of her in-laws than she had ever seen before, some of them for the first time. They came one after the other and shook their heads gloomily over his bed, but few of them offered to keep watch over him through the night. Geini and Betsan the oldest sister were especially good in this respect, and William lived too far away to stay. As for the others, they came and spread their wings over the bed as if they wanted to keep Jane from coming too near the sick man. They looked as if they were laying siege to a city, and Jane was glad to see the back of them. Sioned Gruffydd seemed to relish her sadness and went about like a ship in full sail. If anyone happened to meet her outside the door as she was leaving, this is what Jane heard,

"I am his mother," in a melancholy voice.

Jane and Geini, and Jane and Betsan, kept watch, and Bob Ifans, Twnt i'r Mynydd, and some of the neighbours came. They applied a linseed poultice every two hours. One night, when Ifan was very ill, the sweat pouring from him, his breath coming in short gasps, immediately after a bad bout of coughing, the door and window wide open, and Geini fanning him, Edward, his brother came to see how he was. Jane had not seen this brother before, but his manner in the bedroom was as if he had come into his own house.

"Why don't you move that table away from the window so that he can get more air?" he said.

"You could have done that if you'd come here sooner," said Geini.

Seeing him move towards the table, Jane said, "No, it's better to leave it now, the noise will disturb him."

Edward stared at the ceiling which was very near his head, as if he was going to move that as well.

"If you want to do something, sit in this chair," said Jane, who had felt for a long time that her husband's family was a bit too much for the place. If Ifan was going to die, her one wish was to be alone with him. She did not want even Geini's company. She felt her love flooding out towards her husband, and she would not have the chance to say anything of what she felt in the company of these family witnesses.

After she had gone into the kitchen, Edward lowered his voice and asked Geini, "Has he made a will?"

"Hush," she said, with such force that the sick man turned his head with a moan and licked his dry lips.

"Jane," he said, "a drink." She ran to the kitchen and gave it to him.

The next night he was worse, and they sent for his mother. But in the middle of the night, about two in the morning, he became quiet. Sioned Gruffydd sat by the fire, sleeping, Bob Ifans and Betsan were in the bedroom. Jane moved quietly between the bedroom and the kitchen fire. At last she sat down in front of the fire. The kettle sang quietly on the hob. From the back-bedroom came the snores of one of the children. Occasionally the sick man complained. The clock ticked away. Embers fell from the kitchen grate. The night was heavy, and Jane fell asleep despite her anxiety. Sleep was stronger than her love.

She was awakened by Ifan's voice calling her name. "Jane," he said, "where are the children?"

That was the first sign that he was getting better.

For Jane the months following were happy ones despite her load of troubles.

She was like someone saved from a sinking ship. Material things faded into insignificance – the great thing was to be alive. All the money troubles associated with building the new extension were of no importance when her husband began to get better. But now she had to do something she had never done before – ask for credit at the shop. There was no other way out. Ten shillings a week was all she had from the sickness club. Strangely enough, she had worried more about money matters and things like that before Ifan became ill. She had felt that they had taken too much on themselves, and feared a drop in wages. Her husband would not be able to work for weeks, the money from the club would be cut, and after that he would not be able to work at full pace. But now that the burden was on her she threw the weight of it off and refused to think about it. It was enough for her that Ifan was alive. Nothing else could trouble her.

Her mother came to visit Ifan. She asked nothing about their circumstances and Jane told her nothing. But her mother gave her a sovereign before she left. This desire to help came to her, not so much at seeing her son-in-law looking so grey and thin, but through pity that her daughter had to live in such a poor area. True, it was the beginning of winter, but the woman of Sarn Goch could not imagine anything growing in that bleak countryside, even in summer.

CHAPTER SIX

A few months after Ifan had started working again, their third child, Wiliam, was born and two years later came another son, Owen, and the parents had a glimpse of the day when the boys would be of help to them after they had started working in the quarry. Wiliam looked as if he would develop into a strong lad, but Owen was a bit of a weakling, although capable of learning everything.

One evening in January 1893 there was a children's meeting at the chapel and the four children were there. It was to chapel that the children usually went. They attended all the weekly meetings, and their mother now went to chapel more often than to church, when she could go. It was a clear moonlit night and everything underfoot was frozen. Before going to the chapel the children used to slide on the streams that ran straight down from the fields to the gully of the river that ran through the village – if you can call a yard-wide stream a river. On cold days the children used to run home at full speed although they were tempted to slide on the way up. But it was better to rush home, have a meal and then go and slide afterwards. On these short winter days they wouldn't have a proper tea but a basin of broth instead, since it was so near the time for a quarryman's supper – usually stew, in winter. The boys would eat standing up without taking their coats off so that they could hurry out again. Afterwards, they would all have to help, the girls to wash up and the boys to fetch heather and coal ready to light the fire in the morning. These were their usual chores after coming home from school.

"Now then," said their mother, emphasising the 'then', "if you are not coming home before the meeting, you will have to have a wash now. Owen, take that scarf off so that you can have a really good wash."

Owen scowled. He thought he would have been able to run out to slide as soon as he'd done his chores. But in a trice he was ready, his face shining red, and a lock of wet, unruly hair standing straight up by the peak of his cap. He re-wound the big scarf round his neck so that only his nose and eyes could be seen. The boys wore short, double-breasted coats – monkey jackets. The girls wore short coats, something similar, over their aprons. Round their necks they wore white furs like sheep's tails, tied under their chins by ribbons, and they had caps like those of the boys on their heads.

There was a full moon in the sky, almost as yellow as a September one. The cold wind pierced the children's clothes, and water came from their eyes and noses in drops. As they went they sang, or chanted to a tune:

> *Lleuad yn ola,*
> *Plant bach yn chwara,*
>
> *Lladron yn dwad,*
> *Dan weu sana,*
> *"A-men" meddai'r ffon,*
> *Dwgyd teisus o siop John.*
> *John, John, gymi di gin,*
> *Cyma, cyma, os ca'i o am ddim.*

(Moon shining,
Children playing,
Here come thieves,
All a-knitting.
"A-men", said the sticks
Stealing cake from Dick's,
Dick, Dick, have a stout,
Yes, yes, if I have it for nowt.)

All the children attending the meeting were sliding above the stream, everybody anxious to go on the slide. They could not wait for one to go whilst the others watched. One after the other they went, and the thing to do was to leave the slide before it descended into the gully. The boys did this by turning their bodies from one side to the other and raising their arms to steer themselves. But the girls tended to keep their hands in their pockets and so found it more difficult to turn from the slide before the end. Owen tried to do the same as the girls, but his trick failed and he was forced to jump over the river to the other side of the gully. His feet hit the hard ground so heavily that the pain shot through his body like thousands of needles, and he felt he had landed on his head rather than his feet. No-one had time to see if he had hurt himself. He ran back up the gully to a place where he could cross and so return to the slide.

"You silly fool," one of his mates said to him. "Why didn't you raise your arms?"

"I wanted to jump across", he replied.

"You watch that you don't land in the middle of the river," said another voice.

The words 'silly fool' cut Owen deeply. He could not forget them nor the tone in which they were said. He could not bring himself to go on the slide again. The fact was that he hadn't wished to jump the gully, but he had been almost flung over by the crowd of hefty lads coming behind him, and he such a small boy. He had felt as if he were about to be pushed over the edge and thought the best thing to do was to jump clear, and he felt he had done rather a memorable thing in clearing the gully. The other boys and girls continued to slide one after the other without stopping or tiring and with their arms raised and bodies aslant they looked like flying swallows.

Before long, Elin noticed that Owen was not sliding.

"Why have you stopped?", she asked.

Owen did not answer.

"Now then, come on, don't be so silly."

"I am not silly," he said hotly, "and I'll show you I'm not, too."

He took a run and off he went on the slide, and because the others had been listening to him and Elin, they had stopped for a moment, and so he had the slide to himself. Skimming along as light as a feather, he managed to turn off before reaching the bottom. He was cheered and clapped.

Later on, at the meeting, everybody was surprised to see Owen entering nearly every competition. The chapel was cold after the sliding. They arrived, a noisy troop with red hands and faces. Only the lamps in the lower part were lit, and the long shadows of the children were thrown into the unlit part, and only half the Superintendent's face could be seen in the deacon's pew.

"You're not coming!" said Sioned, when she saw Owen going to the porch during the competition for putting words into correct Welsh.

"Yes I am," said Owen, putting his cap into his pocket.

"What do you know about it?" said William. "You're far too young."

"You'll soon see," said Owen.

The porch was dark and the older children welcomed the opportunity to pinch and stick pins into each other, and when a man came to look after them they stuck a pin in him too. He put out his arm and clouted the boy nearest him. Owen crouched among the other children, his heart beating with expectation. Every kind of sensation went through him, and one moment he would swallow his spit and the next moment he felt so light-headed he felt he would faint. Suddenly the door opened and the light fell on the faces of those children nearest to it.

"Next," said a voice, and Owen slid inside.

"Well, the little devil," said a boy from behind, "that was

my turn."

Owen went up to the deacon's pew, afraid that he wouldn't be able to say a word. But when the man said, "Give me the proper Welsh word for 'iwsio', "Defnyddio", was Owen's bullet-like reply.

"Cabaits"... "Bresych."

"Trowsus"... "Llodrau."

"Stesion" ... "Gorsaf."

And so Owen went on to the end, correct each time. The same thing happened in the competition for reading an unpunctuated passage; for directing a stranger; and for reciting. Owen won them all and he went home with thirteen pennies clinking in his pocket.

He raced home with the metal rim of his clog in his pocket; it had come off during the sliding. But his face fell when he saw there was a stranger in the house. He should have remembered that, Ann Ifans, Twnt i'r Mynydd, frequently called there when there was a children's meeting. She came to escort the children to the chapel and then stayed with Jane and Gruffydd until they came home. The Twnt i'r Mynydd children had their supper with those of Ffridd Felen. Owen wanted the house to himself to tell his parents about his victories.

"Where are the other children?" was his mother's first question.

"They're coming," he said.

If only his mother had asked, "Well, what did you do at the meeting?" he would have had a good chance to give them his news. But to Owen it seemed obvious that his mother did not think he was capable of winning anything. Since he was the fourth child he had learned to read under the noses of the older ones and they did not notice his precocity, for they were quick themselves.

The others at last trooped into the house.

"Heavens above, Owen has fooled us all tonight."

The three adults turned their heads in amazement.

"He has won everything except the singing."

"How much money did you get?" asked John, Twnt i'r Mynydd.

"One and a penny." said Owen, shyly, "and I've lost the metal rim off my clog."

Everybody laughed except his father.

"Drat it," he said, for he liked nothing worse than having to search for his box of nails just before going to bed. Owen felt some of the pleasure oozing away from his one and a penny as he heard his father grumbling to himself whilst nailing the clog. But everything was fine afterwards as the children ate their supper of tea and bread and butter and cheese, his father smiling with all the others.

Ann Ifans was an easy-going, humorous woman, and while the children had been at the chapel she had regaled Jane and Ifan with her witty stories. Her chief complaint against life was that she had been shut away from civilisation. What she really meant was that she was cut off from the village whenever it snowed. The hedges would be the paths to her house on those occasions. Her greatest pleasure was to have company. A moonlit night was as good as a present to her. Hardly anything troubled her. She turned a prophetic eye on the children as they ate.

"There's no knowing what these children will be some day. Perhaps Owen here will be a banker."

All the children laughed, remembering the money Owen had in his pocket.

"He is beginning to bank already," said John.

"His mother has plenty of places to put those pennies," said his father.

Owen frowned.

"Don't worry, Owen," said Ann Ifans, "perhaps you'll be a millionaire one day, riding in a coach, your mother wearing a veil."

33

After the Twnt i'r Mynydd family had gone, his mother asked Owen,

"Don't you want to give the money to your mother?"

"No," said Owen defiantly. The mother looked at the father, and the father looked at Owen, in a manner that seemed to indicate that the latter had sinned against the Almighty.

"Give them to your mother, and no nonsense," said his father.

"There's plenty of need to buy food for you."

"I want to buy a copy-book, a rubber and pencil with them," said Owen.

"It's more important for you to have food than things like that," said his mother.

Owen flung the pennies on the table in a fit of temper, and his mother boxed his ears. He burst into tears and, sobbing, went to bed. He cried for a long time after putting his head on the pillow.

"Stop your howling," said Wiliam. "I want to go to sleep."

He continued to cry quietly then.

"There you are," whispered someone at his head after a while, "don't take it so hard, I'll buy you a copy-book." It was Elin, having run there in her nightgown when she heard him crying. She was not at all sure of getting a penny, but she thought it was worth promising him one. This promise pacified Owen because there was at least one person in the house who understood this desire.

This was the first time he had come into the real struggle that went on in the home against poverty. He had no idea at all where his food and clothes came from. Day after day they arrived and he never thought from where. He failed to see how his little bit of prize-money could buy much food for anyone. His sorrow was boundless. He kept catching his breath and sighing deeply. This was the first time he had been really sad, and it was such an unexpected sorrow. His feelings had been hurt on the slide, but his triumphs at the children's meeting had wiped that from his memory. He had run home thinking of the welcome he would have and how pleased his parents would be because he wanted to buy a copy-book instead of sweets. He had not expected this. He had felt happy, too, whilst having supper because he was so fond of Ann Ifans and her children. She had such cheerful blue eyes and was always ready with a funny story. Her children were not great learners but they were great admirers of anybody who could learn. He had enjoyed the way Ann Ifans looked at him during supper.

But now all his happiness was in ruins. His father was in a bad temper because he had to repair his clog and his mother had cuffed him because he had thrown the money on the table. And he had beaten children older than himself in every competition! No word from anybody about that except for the unspoken ones in Ann Ifans' eyes.

Very often recently he had noticed his mother looking sad. She was sad when the pigs went away. Owen could not understand that because she would be getting money for them (which was always kept in a special box). But his mother complained that the price of pigs dropped every time she had a cartload to send away. "If I had sold them a fortnight ago I would have had fourpence ha'penny instead of fourpence farthing." And then there was that day the calf died; his mother wept. She was terribly sad again later on when they had to sell a young cow to the butcher because she had only three teats. Owen failed to understand what difference one missing teat made to a cow if she had a good udder. And, after all, they were paid for that cow, but Owen heard them say that they had to throw away good money to buy another.

He remembered asking his mother one day,

"Mam, what if there wasn't anything?"

"What do you mean?"

"What if there was nothing, nothing there (pointing to the sky), or nothing anywhere and we weren't here either?"

"It would be marvellous, my boy," was her only reply.

He had come to associate his mother's sad looks with all grown-ups. But no, Ann Ifans was different.

Owen had been puzzled by things, and that night in bed he began to realise that his mother's reply had something to do with the fact that she did not have enough money to buy food. But everything seemed so confused, and he fell asleep.

In her bedroom the mother regretted having treated Owen so harshly. She should have been proud that he had won so many prizes, showing he had a good head on his shoulders. She should have dealt with him patiently instead of flying off the handle like that. It would not have been difficult, for Owen was the only one of the older children to cling to his mother. But the long, constant struggle to survive had made her short-tempered. Ifan slept the heavy sleep of the quarryman.

Next morning, Owen was almost his old self, but sometimes a pang of memory came. As he was going through the gate on his way to school, his mother called to him and gave him three pennies.

"There you are," she said, "buy a copy-book and such things with these. You'll have some better ones another time."

Owen was too shy to show his joy, but there was a light in his eyes as he said, "I'll come to chapel with you on Sunday night."

CHAPTER SEVEN

In the year 1899 Owen won a scholarship to the County School. This was quite an achievement for only six scholarships were awarded in those days, and he had to compete against the town children, and had to write in English. Owen had set his heart on going to the County School, but after sitting the examination he felt he did not stand a chance. He was one of those children who do not do justice to themselves in examinations. For months before, he had worried, not about the examination itself, but about the details surrounding it. How he would go to the school, where to sit, how to ask for more paper. He did not sleep much the night before. He envied the nonchalant attitude of the other boys as they strolled to the town that morning. But, as he found out many times later in life, it was not half as bad as he had expected.

One Saturday afternoon towards the end of July it was rumoured in the district that he had won a scholarship. The news was brought by the brake driver. The brake ran to the town three times a week. On Saturday it made four journeys, and when it approached noon, Morgan Huws, the coachowner, told somebody that he had spoken to somebody who had heard from the County School governors' clerk that Owen headed the list of successful candidates. Owen heard about it somewhere in the village and he dashed home. He collapsed into a chair; to have his dreams come true at the first attempt was too much for him.

There was nobody in the house but his mother, and when she heard the news she was struck dumb, because for many years things had gone more against her than for her. Momentarily, she could not take in what had happened. When she began to understand, so many things went through her mind that she was unable to speak. One moment she felt full of joy that it was her son who had won the scholarship; the next moment her heart sank when she thought that Ifan might be disappointed. The wages in the quarries were very low at this time and every father looked forward to the time when his son would be going to the quarry with him. It dawned on her, too, that Owen would cost a great deal more in the County School than in the Elementary School.

Her meditations were interrupted.

"Aren't you pleased, mam?"

"Yes, but I'm considering."

"Considering what?"

"What will your father say?"

"What can he have to say?"

"He can make you go to the quarry."

This possibility had not dawned on Owen.

"Why?"

"Perhaps we won't be able to afford to send you to the County School."

"But it will cost nothing since I've won the scholarship."

"Yes but you see perhaps your father will want you to go to the quarry to earn some money."

Owen was dumbfounded. He had never thought that anybody could object to his going. Once again his heart sank when he saw himself face to face with what he later called 'a money problem.'

His father returned home and did not appear any more pleased than his mother. He tended to doubt the truth of the news. The mother stirred herself.

"Ifan," she said, "go to town to find out if it is true. It's quite a time since you were there. You go too, Owen."

"No, I don't want to go," said Owen.

"You don't want to go to town?"

"No, I'd rather stay at home. Perhaps the news isn't true."

Under different circumstances, Owen would have jumped at the offer. But going to town to ask about something that could turn into a disappointment was a far cry from going there on Ascension Thursday when his father's Club paraded, and seeing the band marching, and having more than a halfpenny to spend, the most he was allowed to spend on the way to school. To stay at home, too, was unpleasant. He would have to wait hours before receiving certain knowledge.

He went into the field and lay on his back with his face to the sun. He began to think things over. The night of the children's meeting came back to him, when he was cuffed for throwing the prize money on the table. He had then begun to realise that food and clothing were not to be had for nothing. He remembered Ann Ifans's happy face that night, and the way it contrasted with his mother's. He was bitterly disappointed that nobody seemed very glad that he had won the scholarship.

Somehow, nobody showed much joy over anything in his house. Wil was too tired when he came home from the quarry. His feet dragged as he neared the house in his hobnailed boots and his corduroy trousers hung limply about him. Perhaps it would be better if he went to the quarry like Wil. It would be easier in the long run. Wil had a good head on his shoulders, but probably, he would have to work in the quarry all his life. It was not fair that he, Owen, should have a chance denied to his brother. But, finally, he had to make his own way: he had to go to the County School.

Between the heat and his anxiety, he was sweating. He turned his face away from the sun. The ground, hot underneath him, was sweating too. With one eye Owen could see the young grass growing green and supple between the hard, dry stubble. The cat came and rubbed her soft fur across his face. The sunlight shone on her fur and penetrated to the skin which was a pale red, like a man's skin when held up to the light. The cat was pressing against him, and he pushed her away. She circled around as if not knowing what to do, the pieces of hay making her walk affectedly. She returned once more and turned her head lovingly towards his face.

He sat up. The countryside was lovely around him. The sea was blue, and Anglesey seemed far away with a light haze resting on her. There, red on the horizon, was the County School. Beside it was Llanfeuno Cemetery with the sunlight glancing off its marble tombstones, making them sparkle like diamonds. The fields around him were quiet and dreamlike and at that moment Owen loved them. He had always loved them. He realised that, from now on he would not be able to spend as much time on Ffridd Felen land. There in the bottom corner of the field was a blackberry bush. He remembered the thrill of delight that went through him when he first came across those blackberries, and afterwards learned that they were like cultivated ones, only smaller. On his left was the bilberry bush standing out as a green smudge against the yellow of gorse and the purple heather. The bilberries attracted much attention in June and July.

He remembered that his mother had made a bilberry tart for tea. But the house was hot; his mother had been baking that morning and roasting the meat for Sunday. It had been like a furnace at dinnertime. Nevertheless, he went back to the house. His father would not be home for a long time yet. The tea was on the table and Wiliam was already eating, having changed his clothes. He looked less tired in his best suit and starched collar. It was hot enough to cause Owen to remove his indiarubber collar. Wiliam was having his tea early so that he could go out with his friends.

"You'll have your tea now with me," said his mother to Owen.

The kitchen was cooler by now, with only a faint glow of cow-dung from the fire; the kettle was coming slowly to the boil on it.

"Where are Twm and Bet?" asked Owen.

"Gone up the mountain to gather bilberries with the Manod children," answered his mother.

"Are you tired, my boy?" she added, seeing how flushed his face was.

"It's because I've been lying in the sun. When will father be home?"

"Not for hours yet, you'll have to be patient."

And oddly enough, from that moment he was able to give up thinking about the scholarship. He always felt happy when his mother was friendly like this. The tea was good, especially the bilberry tart. The house, too, was pleasant, the oak furniture shining, the loaves of bread set on the floor to cool, the traces of the smell of baking still lingering in the air. His mother wore a cotton lilac-patterned dress and Owen thought how well she looked in it. Her hair appeared darker somehow and her skin whiter. Why couldn't his home always be like this? By now the question of the scholarship had faded into insignificance. He felt kindly disposed towards everybody, especially his mother.

Shortly, Twm and Bet arrived home and a few bilberries in the bottom of a pitcher. Twm was seven, and Bet four. Jane Gruffydd had had a reasonable interval between Owen and Twm. As they were eating, Aunt Geini bustled into the house.

"Is it true?" were her first words.

"I don't know," said Jane, "Ifan has gone to town to find out."

"Oh, I do hope it is," said Geini, too excited almost to sit down.

"If it's true, I doubt very much if we'll be able to afford to send him to school after all."

"What! Certainly you will. It would be a sin to hold the boy back."

"But he would be able to earn something in the quarry with his father, and you know how difficult it is, paying for this house."

41

"But he'll bring in more money when he's finished his schooling."

"I doubt it."

"Yes, I will," said Owen.

To the two women there was something very endearing about Owen at that moment. As for him, he could have hugged his Aunt Geini for sticking up for him.

"I'm expecting Sioned back any minute," said his mother.

"Oh, now you mention it," said Geini, "I met her just now going to mother's and she told me to tell you not to expect her. She will have supper with mother."

Jane Gruffydd wrinkled her brows; Sioned was almost seventeen and in a sewing school in Pont Garrog. She had gone into service after leaving school the same as her sister, Elin, but she did not get on with the two mistresses, and she said she wanted to become a sempstress. In this she was supported by her grandmother. Sioned Gruffydd had begun to take an interest in her grand-daughter at the time of Ifan's illness, and Sioned spent most of her days-off at the Fawnog.

Sixteen years old, she was a tall, beautiful girl with a fair complexion. Her hair was a light amber with wide waves in it. Her eyes were nut-coloured with a tendency to turn upwards at the outer edges. Her skin was like cream with a little red in it. From the time she went as an apprentice she thought of little else but clothes, and when she was not able to persuade her mother to give her money to buy material for a dress, she would wheedle it from her grandmother. Lately, she had been going to her grandmother's instead of coming straight home on a Saturday afternoon. Even when she was at home she seemed to be shut up in another world and had little to say. She was very short with anybody who tried to have a conversation with her.

When she turned up her nose at her breakfast of bread and butter one morning, her mother took the opportunity of doing something she had long wanted to do, to ask her seriously what was the matter with her these last few months.

Sioned flared up and showed plainly enough that she thought herself a cut above the people of Ffridd Felen.

"An old place like this," she said, "cut off from the world, way behind the times, eating the same thing day after day."

Jane Gruffydd was almost too shocked to speak. To think that her own child could say such things! And to tell the truth, Jane prided herself on keeping a good table as a rule.

Without raising her voice, she said, "Perhaps you'll be glad to eat at this table one day. You won't get better food at your grandmother's house, I warrant."

This quarrel cleared the air for a while. But lately Sioned had begun to pay more frequent visits to her grandmother's house again. No wonder, then, that her mother looked so displeased when she heard Geini say that Sioned had gone straight from work to her grandmother's house.

Ifan came home with the eight o'clock brake, and nobody needed to ask whether or not Owen had won the scholarship. The father seemed absolutely delighted and his eyes were sparkling. To Owen, his eyes seemed to have a tendency to squint. There was a red band on his forehead where his hat had been and the sweat gathered in drops on his forehead. The house smelt differently somehow, a smell which Owen could not identify.

In the brake going down, Ifan had an idea how to find out if the news was true or not. Elin was a maid with a lawyer in the town, and Ifan thought the lawyer would certainly know.

And so it turned out. Elin was the first member of the family to exult in the achievement, and she managed to convince her father that it would be foolish for Owen to go to the quarry instead of to the school.

Later on, in the square, Ifan met one of his mates from the quarry, Guto Cerrig Duon, and the two of them went to 'The Fox and Horses', to celebrate the news by buying each other a pint of beer.

Leaving the pub, he came face-to-face with Doli Rhyd Garreg and her daughter, Gwen. It was impossible to avoid her and, under the influence of the beer and the news, he could not but be agreeable.

Doli wore a little black satin coat that reached a bit below her waist. On her head she had a black toque with little black things like herring scales shining on it. Both she and her daughter had a prosperous look about them, the latter wearing an expensive Leghorn hat and a red French merino dress.

"Just heard this minute the good news about your boy," said Doli.

(In fact she had heard early that morning, for it was that that had brought her to town.)

"Yes," said Ifan, so that the whole square resounded, "he came top."

"Yes, first among the boys, wasn't it?" said Doli in velvet tones. "My daughter came fifth."

"Yes, fifth among the girls, wasn't it, and only three boys and three girls will go in for nothing" said Ifan, copying her tone of voice.

"Gwen can go as a fee-payer, and, often enough, ones like Gwen turn out better than the top ones."

"They do. Good afternoon," said Ifan, and away he went for the brake.

While Ifan gave an account of all this, his eyes sparkled with mischief.

"Well," said his wife, "Owen shall go to the County School, if it's only to spite Doli Rhyd Garreg."

"No," said Ifan. "Owen is to go to school to be educated. He'll be able to make his way in the world then, and nobody will be able to take his education away from him."

Ifan had learned a lesson from Elin, and his present attitude was so different from what it was before he went to town that everybody laughed.

"I never heard you talk such sense," said Geini.

Ifan had brought some brawn home for supper and Geini was made to stay.

Nothing troubled them until the father asked, "Where's Sioned?"

"Over with mother," said Geini. "There's no need for you to keep any of this brawn; she will have had her supper." Jane hid her face so that no-one could see her expression.

About ten o'clock Sioned returned home, her face flushed and her eyes shining. She was dripping with sweat after running, but there was a light in her eyes such as is seen only in the eyes of those who are in love for the first time. She had left her grandmother's at six o'clock and gone to meet Dic Edwards, a shopkeeper from the town, in the Ceunant woods. She had sacrificed supper for that, and in bed she turned and tossed until the small hours of the morning as she re-lived the events of the evening.

In her own bed, the mother was for a long time trying to fathom the reason for the happy expression on Sioned's face.

In his bed, Owen thought of his father and his tendency to squint, and he laughed. Then he thought of the change that had taken place within a few hours in his father's opinion of his scholarship. Yes, certainly, adults were very strange people, turning and changing every minute. Then he remembered how pretty Sioned had looked as she came into the house.

Wiliam snored beside him. Only he and the little ones fell asleep that night without thinking.

CHAPTER EIGHT

Six weeks later, Geini got married suddenly without letting anybody in the district know. By this time she was thirty-five and nobody thought she would marry. She had been keeping company with Eben, Ffynnon Oer, for many years, but she had not been able to marry, for, like her brother many years before, she could not leave her mother. It wasn't that Eben did not ask her, but every time matters came to a head, Geini would not make a definite promise. But something had now happened which made her decide at once.

Ever since that Saturday night when Sioned started meeting Dic Edwards, she had been going to her grand-mother's house more often. One day she asked if she could sleep there the following night. The grandmother readily agreed, and by the time Sioned arrived home in Ffridd Felen, she had concocted a good story to tell her mother, that she wished to sew and alter some old clothes for her grandmother. Her mother gave her consent half-heartedly, for she suspected that something was going on. She wanted to go up to Fawnog to find out what Sioned was up to, but that was no good because she knew that Sioned Gruffydd would side with her grand-daughter. Jane's intuition told her that the grandmother was getting her own back by assisting and encouraging Sioned. Every day she wished that Geini would come down so that she could talk it over with her, but she did not come.

Sioned met her lover every night and arrived home very late at her grandmother's house with the story that she had had to work late because the sempstress was very busy. After the first few nights Geini began to doubt the truth of this story. Neither Whitsun nor Easter was approaching and it was not the beginning of Winter. She longed to go down to the sempstress' house, but that would be too much like sneaking, and what if Sioned was telling the truth? The whole thing made her dispirited. Geini's relationship with her mother had never been tranquil. They habitually disagreed, quarrelled, sulked, then returned to speaking terms again. And then it would be wrong to say that harmony was restored, for there was no harmony before. But in every quarrel they had been on equal terms. It did not matter which of the two had the last word they both received equal support from outside. Neither could complain about that.

But now there was a cuckoo in the nest. It would have been easy for Geini to put up with it if only Sioned had shown some signs of friendship. No, she hardly spoke to her. She slept with her grandmother, which was something unhealthy in Geini's eyes. Sioned must have something to hide. She set off in the morning in her black working dress with a parcel under her arm but returned at night wearing her best dress, again with a parcel under her arm. Geini thought it a sin that she should wear her best dress every day – a light purple one, trimmed with a slightly darker ribbon crinkled at the wrists and in a semi-circle across the breast. The bodice was of white satin covered with lace and the neckband was the same. The dress was getting too short for her. She wondered, did her mother know that Sioned was wearing her best dress every day? She wanted to go over to Ffridd Felen, but she might put her foot in it. She did not want to cause trouble if it was possible to avoid it. She might even cause bad feeling between Ifan and Jane.

However, the morning of the fourth day she could stand it no longer. She had been out feeding the pigs and chickens after milking, and was returning to the house for breakfast. Sioned had just finished her own breakfast of tea, bread and butter, and an egg, and was looking at herself in the mirror before setting off. Geini saw her mother getting some money from her purse in the drawer of the dresser. Sioned went out through the door and her grandmother followed, and Geini knew that money had changed hands. This infuriated her. She thought of the previous night, and Sioned sitting in the armchair like a great lady with her legs stretched out across the hearth. She rattled the dishes and made a clatter as she prepared her own breakfast.

"Why are you losing your temper?"

"I should like to know what you were giving to Sioned."

"Is it anybody else's business what I was giving to her?"

"Yes, it's my business."

"Since when?"

"Since I've been working and slaving here. It's a fine state of affairs for me to be making the money, and you giving it to something like that."

"If you don't like it, you know what to do."

"Yes, and I know what you will have to do too."

"Sioned will come and stay with me."

Geini burst out laughing.

"I can just see that lady giving the calves their mash!"

That evening Geini went to Eben and told him that she wished to marry him.

On the way back she called at Ffridd Felen. She had decided to tell the parents everything about Sioned. But she was spared that. There had been a commotion there ever since Ifan came home from the quarry.

Morus Ifan, a Little Steward by this time, husband of Doli Rhyd Garreg, had called Ifan into the office at the quarry. Buckley, the Steward, was not there.

Little Steward is a title given to an under-Manager, but Morus Ifan was little in every respect. Even his abilities as a Steward were so limited that he was afraid of losing his job, and as usual with a man like that, he kept a tight rein on the men. He was afraid of the workmen because he feared his own shortcomings. But he worked hand-in-glove with the

Steward and so played into the hands of the owners. Ifan's life at the quarry had not been a happy one ever since the Little Steward married Doli. He had not tried to persecute him, but Ifan always felt in his presence that it was like playing with a little cat's paws. They were as soft as velvet, but the claws could be suddenly extended. And this day Ifan thought he was going to see the claws.

"Sit down, Ifan Gruffydd," said Morus Ifan.

Ifan did so, placing his hard, dusty hat on his knee.

"What I have to say to you has nothing to do with the quarry," said the Little Steward, who was playing with his watch-chain. "I feel I ought to tell you about the behaviour of Sioned, your daughter."

"Sioned! What has Sioned been doing?"

"Well, I hate having to tell you, but I have seen her two or three times lately with some boy in the Ceunant woods."

"Are you sure, because she goes straight from work to my mother's at the Fawnog to sew for her, and she sleeps there afterwards."

The Steward smiled knowingly, like one used to the tricks of young people courting. Ifan saw that and blushed.

"Was she doing anything wrong?" was his next question.

"Oh no, but I thought you would be pleased to know that your girl, and she so young, was sitting in the Ceunant woods with a young man's arm around her waist."

Ifan was ready with a sharp reply when he remembered that he was only a worker and the other was an official, and times were bad.

"Thank you for letting me know," said Ifan courteously, and left the office.

The Steward felt disappointed after Ifan had left. He had expected Ifan to answer him back, and then he would always have had a hold on him.

This happened just on knocking-off time, and Ifan did not have to face any of his work-mates with this weight on his mind. On the way home he answered his companions with his lips, but he was seething inside. Why hadn't he given the interfering little sneak a piece of his mind? If he had been going for a stroll through the Ceunant woods the first evening he saw Sioned there, Ifan was certain that he went there again to peep on her. And yet, it was for the best that he managed to hold his tongue. Wages were low and it was a great favour that he was allowed extra time to work for his son these days. The Steward could sack him, and he and the Little Steward were hand-in-glove. But Oh! Ifan was ashamed of himself. If one of his workmates had told him about Sioned it would have been with the best intentions, but he knew that the Little Steward took a delight in humiliating Ifan.

Then he turned his attention to Sioned. What was to be done with her? He, himself, had not been much older when he had started courting Doli. He could not blame her for courting. Yet she was very young, and times were changing. In Ifan's time a youngster would be earning enough to keep a wife, before reaching today's school leaving-age. But it was Sioned's deceitfulness he did not like. She went to her grandmother's house too often as it was, without using it as a refuge from her parents' eyes.

He sighed as he hung his hat on the nail, and Jane knew at once that something was wrong.

After they had finished the quarryman's meal, his mother told Owen, "Go and call on Twnt i'r Mynydd, you haven't been there for some time."

Usually he would have jumped at the chance of going there, but now he knew that there was something brewing and that he was being sent out of the way. Twm and Bet had not returned from their wanderings. They would hardly be seen all day during the long summer holidays. Of the children, only Owen and Wiliam were there. Owen set off unwillingly, dragging his feet.

"Can I wear my best boots; I'm tired of these."

"Yes," said his mother, feeling a wave of pity for him.

Then in the presence of Jane and Wiliam, Ifan gave an account of what the Little Steward had told him.

Having suspected something for some time, the mother was not all that surprised. What made her angry was that it had gone on for such a long time, since Sioned had had a bolt-hole in the form of her grandmother's house. If she had tried to fool them at home, she would have been caught a long time ago.

"We are very much to blame for letting your mother keep her for so long," said Jane.

"Yes," said Ifan impatiently, "but it was Sioned who chose to go there."

"Ay, like a calf after sugar," she said.

"She went there without sugar this time," said Ifan.

For a moment he felt angry with Jane for making out that his mother was more to blame than Sioned.

For him, something like this was a heaviness of heart which destroyed the peace of a man's life. It dawned on him that children were more trouble than they were worth. All he wanted out of life was enough work with good stones in the quarry, a chance to potter about the house after coming home, a newspaper to read and a pipe to smoke before going to bed. But ever since the children had started growing up, they were a constant source of worry. As soon as they were old enough to wander over the threshold there was no knowing from which direction trouble would come. What weighed heaviest on his mind was how he was going to go to his mother's house to fetch Sioned. He was one of those men whose bodies can endure any amount of hard work, and he could cope with any difficulties in the quarry, but all the fibre was knocked out of him once anything came to weigh on his mind.

He went to tidy-up around the haystack. It would be useless to go to his mother's house until much later. About

51

half-past-eight Geini arrived, looking agitated.

"Where's Ifan?" were her first words to Jane.

"He's tidying the haystack," she replied quietly, beetling her brows. "Doing something to pass the time. He wants to go up there soon."

Geini saw that the storm had begun to break.

"He's going there about Sioned?"

"Yes."

"It's about her I've come to talk to you."

"So you've heard the story."

"What story?"

"That she has been meeting a boy in the Ceunant woods."

"Oh, that's what she has been up to is it?"

"You knew nothing about it, then?"

"No, all I know is that she arrives there late, treats me like dirt, and has money from my mother. I've had a bellyful of it. I'm not going to put up with it any longer. Eben and I are going to get married."

"Geini!"

At that moment Ifan came into the house.

"Don't you think I have waited long enough?"

"Yes," replied Ifan, "so long that I can hardly bear to hear the news. What will your mother do?"

"Only what every mother has to do. I've reached the end of my tether."

Ifan sighed. One trouble after another.

"Have you told mother?" was Ifan's question.

"No. You can tell her since you are going there to fetch Sioned."

"No. No. I won't, and that's final. It will be enough for me to talk about Sioned."

"You might as well throw in my news at the same time."

Geini laughed, and the others stared in amazement at her seeming lack of concern.

"Now," said Geini, "come on: the sooner you get it over

with, the better." Geini knew her brother well. To her, life for a long time had been a matter of surmounting difficulties, and once you had arrived safely on the other side of one sea of troubles, there was sure to be another waiting for you.

As they drew near Y Fawnog, Ifan felt as he had often felt when nearing home. It was exactly like this that he felt when he had been out courting, like a child dreading a scolding from his mother. He was always afraid that she would fly at him like a cat, for her temper was always uncertain every night he went courting.

"Here's a stranger," were his mother's first words. And that was true. Nowadays, he rarely went to his mother's house, except when they were gathering hay or lifting potatoes. The house was exactly the same as it had always been. Nothing ever changed there except perhaps a new oilcloth on the table or a mat at the hearth. There, as ever, was the round stone carried some time or other by someone from the beach and varnished black. It was placed on the corner of the low garden wall. It was like some eternal sign. Ifan's eyes would alight on it as he raised the latch on the door after an evening's courting. Ever since his marriage he had looked for it each time he went to Y Fawnog. It was there tonight in its place, as ever, and as he passed it on his way to the house, he felt exactly the same as he had felt a hundred times before marrying. In fact everything seemed the same, only now it was because someone else had been courting.

Ifan plunged straight in. "Where's Sioned?"

"She's working late, isn't she?"

"Yes, so she says, and you say."

"Who says differently?"

"Those who have seen her with a young man in Ceunant Woods."

His mother's face fell, and she went to sit by the fire, fumbling with the edges of her shawl.

"Who are they then?" was her next question.

"Well, it was Morus Ifan who told me."

His mother was silent. She had a servile respect for the man who had married her son's sweetheart. She kept on fumbling with her shawl. Inside, she was seething with indignation that her grand-daughter had deceived her so. But she also knew that someone else besides Sioned was to blame.

Meanwhile, Geini had been moving about between the bedroom and the kitchen, taking off her hat and coat and putting on her apron. She came to sit at the table, and looked at Ifan to urge him to tell his mother her news.

He, seeing his mother so quiet, thought she was sad, and could not bring himself to make it worse by telling her the other news. What a problem! Talk about Hell! This was worse than the time of his own wedding when Geini had to break his news to his mother. And now here was Geini unable to announce her own wedding. It looked as if it was easier to announce someone else's. Suddenly Sioned Gryffydd said,

"I'm afraid you haven't been treating the girl properly at home."

"Treating? How is she treated differently from the others?"

"You are far too strict with her."

Geini could stand it no longer.

"I'd say she was having far too much of her own way."

"Nobody was speaking to you," said Sioned Gruffydd.

"No, I dare say not," said Geini. "Nobody chooses to speak to me. But I've got a finger in this pie. I'm not going to stay here any longer to be trodden underfoot by you and Sioned. Do you know," she said, turning to Ifan, "I'm not angry with Sioned for sneaking out courting but rather for pretending to be a great lady, turning up her nose at somebody like me who is fool enough to wait on her hand and foot? But," she continued, turning to her mother, and with a trembling voice, "everything comes to an end, and I'm leaving here to get married in three weeks time."

"And good riddance,"said the mother.

"Mother!" said Ifan. "For shame, saying such a thing to someone who has been so good to you."

"Tut," said Geini, "that's nothing to what I usually get."

Ifan felt wretched. There was a sense in which he preferred Geini to anybody except his wife and children, and his relationship with her was different from his relationship with them. This was possibly the most painful experience of his life, to hear his sister, whom he liked so much, running down his own daughter to his face. Life, especially family matters, was becoming more of a tangled mess every moment.

In the middle of the crying and confusion Sioned entered the house. She did not have to ask what was the matter. She looked like a trapped wild bird. Ifan looked at his daughter as if he was getting to know her for the first time. She was like a stranger's child to him. He had never realised that she was so beautiful. She had grown from childhood into a young woman without his knowing.

"You'd better come with me," he told her.

She had to submit to that voice.

Not a word passed between father and daughter on the way back to Ffridd Felen, and not many even after they arrived there. Ifan Gruffydd was a man who found it difficult to chastise, and by this time his wife thought Sioned had been punished enough by being caught. What troubled the mother most was that Sioned had created discord between Geini and Sioned Gruffydd, and this could cause a rift between Geini and herself. One of the most valuable things in Jane's life since coming to live in the district had been Geini's fidelity. She made that perfectly clear to her daughter. Ifan was pleased that his wife was dealing with the situation so capably and showing such good sense by pointing out to Sioned the harm she had done to her Aunt Geini. Ifan was often quite cross with his wife, but there was in her a kind of stability and a sense of what was right that always won his respect. These were the qualities he had liked in her from the beginning, and these he admired in her to her grave.

Sioned herself spoke not a word, and this shortened her mother's sermon. But she burst out crying after a while and agreed to eat her supper.

Nobody learned the meaning of her tears. She was like the doll in the china-cabinet in the best room.

CHAPTER NINE

Geini was married, and she and her husband went to live in a little cottage which was nearer to Ffridd Felen than to Y Fawnog. Eben, her husband, was known to be a careful man, and Geini started her married life with no debts to encumber her. She had to borrow from Jane and Ifan to buy her wedding clothes, but she soon repaid that.

The only thorn in Geini's flesh was her mother. Even so, she felt that the step she had taken had done her a great deal of good. She had lived more in the last month than in her whole life before. And yet she could not get rid of the feeling that she had not done her duty to her mother despite having been with her for a long time. For twenty years or more she had been continually arguing, disagreeing and quarrelling with her mother, day in, day out, and all that time she had told herself that her mother would regret it one day. In her day-dreams she had often imagined the day when she would leave Y Fawnog and so get the upper-hand over her mother. How often she had pictured herself victorious with her foot on the enemy's neck! Now that day had arrived, and how different it was from how she had imagined! Not to Geini was the victory, for the mother seemed indifferent to her fate. Even if she had shown that she cared, that would only have made it difficult for her to leave, so the mother would have triumphed in any case. Although Sioned Gruffydd had to busy herself once again with cows and pigs, she would not admit that that was a burden. If she had been perfectly honest with herself she would have acknowledged the fact that the greatest loss she had suffered was not having anybody to criticise. It was meat and drink to her to scold others while believing in her own perfection.

As for Sioned, her grand-daughter, after finishing her apprenticeship she obtained a position as sempstress in a shop in the town. Her mother was obliged to agree to this arrangement. The only alternative was for her to sew at home, and Jane thought it the better of two evils that Sioned should go to town. Elin would be there to keep an eye on her. Because of the long hours it was necessary for Sioned to take lodgings in the town during the week, and the family found her more agreeable when she came to spend Sunday at home.

Owen started in the County School, and because there was no convenient transport, he had to walk the four miles to school. He had plenty of company, boys working in shops and offices. They all set off punctually every morning and met at various crossroads. If they passed the house of one of the boys, they would whistle before coming to it and the next moment he would be out at the gate. This was the best companionship that Owen had ever known. There was a kind of tacit understanding among them. Nobody discussed it, but it was there all the same. Very rarely did they quarrel though they sometimes fiercely debated such questions as Disestablishment (Owen tended to speak in favour of the Church) or the war in South Africa. But they were as one in their opposition to any of the other groups walking along the road. They would have nothing to do with the girls who went to the schools or the shops of the town. They tended to look down on them, and yet admired them in secret. They would have a cutting remark or witticism for those going in the opposite direction, people from the town with their goods – pedlars, fishmongers, fruitsellers – and these would answer them back on their own terms. They were as one in their approval or disapproval of other groups of people.

They looked down on boys from the town, or 'coves' as they called them. These returned the remark with 'country-bumpkin'. To the town boys, the country boys were ignorant, especially where good manners were concerned, whilst to the country lads, the town boys appeared over-fastidious and more like girls than boys. There was no argument about such matters in the group to which Owen belonged for the next four years. Their verdict on the town boys was unanimous.

Owen forgot many of the things that happened in the County School, but he never forgot the boys who walked to school with them. There was Rhisiart, Allt Ddu, who seemed to walk on tip-toe. He had younger brothers and a thrifty mother, and as a consequence, his trousers were always too large for him, coming down below the knee. He never wore an overcoat yet he never complained of the cold. There was often a mischievous smile on his face, and he was the main-spring of any fun that was going. In every literary competition, he would think up a more humourous pseudo-nym than anyone else, such as "The one who is after the adjudicator's blood" or "The hairy hedgehog" – pseudonyms which would sometimes cost him the prize. Then there was John Twnt i'r Mynydd, a harmless, innocent boy, who washed his face so completely that he always seemed to have a wet hank of hair falling below his cap. And Bob, Parc Glas, a quiet neat boy with red cheeks and a white skin, contributing little to the conversation, but laughing a great deal.

And so life went placidly on for Owen in the County School. The first few weeks (when he found difficulty in getting his tongue round the strange English words when talking to his teachers) were unpleasant ones, he found it difficult to understand voices using an English intonation.

Although he never became fond of the school, he never disliked it either. Returning home in the evening, he felt released from the atmosphere of the school, and yet during the day it was his home environment which seemed the alien one. He had so much homework that he had no time now for those things he used to do at home when he was in the Elementary School, and apart from the few opportunities he would have on a Saturday afternoon or a Sunday, he became a stranger to the smells of cowshed and haystack. He belonged neither to school nor to his home. His work in every subject was of a consistently high standard, and he was near the top of his class all the time.

Two great things happened to him at the school, things that influenced him more than the formal education he received there – falling in love with Gwen, Doli Rhyd Garreg's daughter, and the close bond which developed between him and his brother Twm.

Gwen was in his class, having entered without a scholarship, but having won half the fees later. Very early on in his new life Owen had noticed a little girl who sat at the front of the class and who often turned round to look at him. She had lively blue eyes, short curly auburn hair and rosy cheeks. She was short and rather plump.

One mid-day when Owen was loitering on the playing field after dinner, she came up to him and said,

"Have you done the sums for tomorrow?"

"Yes," said Owen.

"Did the last one come out?"

"Yes."

"I couldn't work it out at all."

And producing a rough-book from somewhere behind her, she showed the place where the difficulty was.

Owen showed her what to do and straight-away worked out the sum.

"You live at Ffridd Felen?"

"Yes."

"I think my mother and father know your father well."

"Do they?"

"Well, you see, my father is the manager in the quarry."

"Oh?"

And that was all that Owen could say. He had never heard his father say enough about the manager for him to feel any kind of respectful awe in the presence of his daughter.

After this, Gwen was forever plaguing him with her difficulties, and she even went so far as to walk home with him one evening, instead of catching the train as usual. Bron Llech, her home, was on the main road, and there was a station there. But she only did that once. His companions made fun of him, and he was forced to tell her. After that she kept away from him for a time, but not for long. She had a way with her. She looked at him in such a manner that he began to suspect that his help was only secondary and that he himself was the main attraction.

One day, Owen spent a considerable time, leaning on a window-sill, trying to explain a problem to her. All this time there was a satisfied smile on her face, and Owen felt that she must be pleased by his kindness. When she joined her playmates in the field, Owen heard them laughing derisively, and he saw Gwen holding out a bag of sweets to the girls. He was cut to the quick, and told himself that she could at least have offered a sweet after all the trouble he had taken. If he had been nearer to the girls, this is what he would have heard:

"You are lucky, Gwen, to have boys to help you and give you sweets." And he would not have heard Gwen offer any correction.

When the first prize-day came, Owen had come top in most of the subjects. He took home the invitation, inscribed in English on gilt-edged card, for his parents. But they, because they could not understand it, put it aside. As the days went by, the children discussed among themselves who was going to come to the meeting, and he was given to understand that Gwen's mother was to be there. That night he asked his mother if she was coming to the ceremony.

"Me?," she said. "What would I be doing in a place like that, not understanding a word of English?"

"Gwen's mother is coming," said Owen.

"And she can't speak a word of English, either," said the father.

61

"Maybe, but she has grand clothes, and she won't have to open her mouth."

"Come on, Mam," said Owen. "I'm going to get more prizes than anybody."

"No, I won't come."

When the day came, Owen felt dreadfully nervous and lonely. He felt that prize-giving, with all its pomp and ceremony, was something for the gentry. He was afraid of stumbling when going up on the stage, and wished that some member of his family were there so that he would have some kind of support. He was loudly applauded as he went up to receive his prizes.

Afterwards people collected in the yard and Owen noticed Gwen standing with her mother and some other women. Gwen had received just the one prize, for being fairly good in every subject, and the women around her were admiring the book. When Gwen saw Owen, she turned her head away, but Owen noticed that one of the women who looked very like Gwen was trying to keep one eye on him and the other on the admiring group surrounding Gwen. She was wearing a sealskin coat and a veil. Owen could not understand why Gwen had averted her eyes, and had not introduced her mother to him. (The woman in the sealskin coat was probably her mother.) But he decided that she had not seen him.

The next day at school she was as cheerful as ever, but after what had happened, Owen could not be easy in her company and kept well clear of her.

Soon Gwen had another boy to help her, and Owen felt jealous. He did not want to help her himself, and yet he did not want anybody else to become equally admired by Gwen. He began to look on the other boy as one who was trespassing on his property, and he soon found himself talking to Gwen instead of avoiding her.

One Saturday afternoon, towards the beginning of May, there was a children's singing festival in one of the chapels near Bron Llech. This was held in turn in three districts. Apart from the singing, the children were tested in their work during the preceding year and prizes were distributed for Scripture Knowledge. For the youngest children to be allowed to go to this meeting was rather like being allowed to go to town for the first time. They never left their village except to go to town at Whitsun or on Ascension Thursday, or to the seaside during August. For the older children, the singing festival had lost much of its original attraction.

Owen had become accustomed to winning prizes. Other people would say, "It's no use anyone competing; Ifan y Fawnog's son always wins."

The only thrill these occasions gave to Owen now came from seeing the children, many of them strangers to each other, singing together. A large crowd always thrilled him. This particular Saturday it was hotter than usual. The chapel windows were open and a gentle breeze carried the distant bleating of sheep down from the mountain.

Gazing through the window, Owen could see the purple face of the quarry. The sun shone on it, and its light was reflected in a circle of individual rays, like the light from the lamp in the chapel during the winter. The questions and answers fell into the background as he fastened his mind on this marvellous light. Suddenly, he was drawn back to the world of the festival with the singing of 'Flowers of Christ' and 'Faithful Warriors'. But when he sat down again, his eyes were drawn to the purple slate, which seemed to glow in his mind.

He then realised that someone between him and the window was turning around and looking at him. The face was somehow familiar to him, but it was only when it smiled that it dawned on him that it was Gwen. It had not been easy for him to recognise her in her best clothes. She wore a blue-grey dress – the colour of the cuckoo – with a lace collar about the throat. She had a straw hat, the colour of cream, with a wreath of blue flowers around its crown. Its brim was wavy and it half-hid her face. That was why Owen had not recognised her before, and that was why he looked at her often before the festival ended. All this gave rise to feelings that he had not associated with her before. As if it was natural for him to do so he hung around outside the chapel instead of going home immediately after the meeting. When Gwen came out, she left the girls she was with and came towards him.

"Hello," she said.

"Hello," he said shyly, rubbing the toe of his boot in the ground and making a small furrow there.

"Are you going home with those girls?" he asked, after a short pause.

At this, one of the girls called, "Gwen, are you coming?"

"Not for a while. You go on. I'll catch you up."

It had got dark by this time, and in the crowd standing about outside the chapel, it was difficult to pick out one from the other.

"Can I see you home?" asked Owen.

"I don't mind," she said, and now it was her turn to feel bashful.

"We'll go across the fields," said Gwen.

"You can show me the way," replied Owen.

He was far too shy to help her across the stiles. In the darkness, everything seemed unreal, and since the paths were strange to him, he felt as if he was moving through a world of shadows.

"This way," Gwen would frequently say, trying to guide him, and at last she had to take hold of his arm. He did not mind that at all. Turning towards her and gazing at her face in the darkness, Owen thought that he had never seen anything more beautiful. But to tell the truth, Gwen was not beautiful. Certainly she had all the individual attributes of beauty – blue eyes, full of life; wavy, auburn hair; a straight nose; a shapely mouth; good teeth and white skin. And yet she was not pretty. It was as if someone had taken bits of a beautiful painting and failed to assemble them into a perfect whole. Yet, that night, looking at her face in the dark, half-shadowed by the enfolding brim of her hat, Owen thought her very beautiful. He loved the feel of her dress on his arm, and the faint smell of her perfume.

"You are very pretty in that hat," said Owen.

"Do you think so? It's a very expensive hat."

"Why do you let that old town boy show you how to do sums?"

"You didn't seem very willing to show me."

"Well, I will be from now on."

When they reached the road, Gwen said, "It would be better for you to go back now, in case someone sees us. You can go this way. Keep straight on and turn left when you reach the mountain."

Owen turned to go. He wanted to kiss her, but was too shy.

"Will you come to meet me somewhere next Saturday night, about eight?"

"Yes," she replied, and ran away as she heard approaching.

Owen ran all the way home and arrived not much later than Twm and Bet.

Because he had brought home many prizes, and because he was regarded as a quiet, dependable boy, nobody questioned him. But Owen was head-over-heels in love.

Every Saturday night for months afterwards, he and Gwen met in the Wern woods, half-way between their respective houses. They were more fortunate than Sioned and Dic Edwards. The first time they met, Owen was disappointed for Gwen had brought her eternal sums with her. "Oh, forget about those. Let's talk," he said.

For a whole week her image had been before his eyes as he did his work. Day-dreaming about her alternated with periods of work. He did not find pleasure in his tasks. He thought about her every minute of the day. There was some relief from the fever in school for she was there in the same room, but back home he would bite his pencil and nails in turn whilst anticipating next Saturday night. Perhaps it was the night and its new experiences which had occupied his mind, and not Gwen. And now the night had come at last with nothing to hinder him for he had lied about his intentions. Yet he had never thought that Gwen would bring her work along with her. To him this night was different from all the others in his life. But Gwen took no notice of his disappointment. She was like a brand new ball, bouncing up after being struck lightly.

"Just these two sums; we'll talk afterwards."

Owen relented.

"There now," he said after finishing, "Throw that old book aside."

She did so with the satisfied smile of one who had had her way.

The two talked shyly, pulling up handfulls of grass and fern from the ground and crumbling them into tiny pieces.

"Where's that hat you wore last Saturday night?" asked Owen.

"I'm not allowed to wear my best hat every night. Why?"

"You looked awfully pretty in it."

"Don't you like this one?"

"Oh, yes, but the other is exceptional."

Gwen appeared to be mollified, and yet not completely satisfied.

Owen did not notice the difference.

"Do you really think I'm pretty?" was her next question.

"Yes, very pretty indeed."

"Do you know, we girls in Form Four have a game in which we tell the truth about each other quite openly."

"Oh, why?"

"To stop us thinking too much of ourselves."

"Go on; I think in your case it would make you think more of yourself."

"No indeed. I was deeply hurt."

"Why?"

"I was told that apart from my clothes I was not pretty."

"Well, they told you lies."

The cold satisfied smile returned to Gwen's face.

And thus they passed the evening, and other evenings like it. After the sun had gone down they would embrace and kiss. But every Saturday night Gwen brought her school-books with her, so that Owen found himself both teacher and lover at the same time.

When the holidays came, they continued to meet, and now Gwen had no excuse for bringing her books with her, but she worried about the results of the exams. Had she passed? When Owen appeared unconcerned, she would sigh and say that it was all-right for him, he was confident of passing.

"No, not as confident as all that," he said. "But there's no point in worrying. Let's talk about something else."

But when he suggested that, he had no idea of what was to come.

"Tell me," said Gwen, "what kind of boy is your brother Wiliam?"

"What do you mean?"

"Is he bad-tempered, or difficult to live with?"

"I don't know. I see very little of him except when I go to bed and he's usually too tired to talk much there. Why do you ask?"

"Oh, nothing really," she said, "but I sometimes hear my father talking about him to my mother."

"Does he say anything bad about him?"

"Oh, no. Not at all. Just that he and you father are excellent workers."

Owen was satisfied. The relationship between Gwen's

father and his father and brother had never before come to his mind.

And so the weeks went by, and the day for the examination results drew near. Owen was afraid that his affair with Gwen might have had a bad effect on his work. But when Saturday night came, he did not worry about that.

Prize-giving day was in October. As usual, Owen brought the gilt-edged invitation card home to his father and mother, and as usual, Jane Gruffydd threw it down on the table.

"No, you must come this time," said Owen.

"Yes, you should go, Jane," said Ifan. "Fair play to the boy. You are as good as the next one."

"Yes, do come, Mam. I've got the best certificate of all in the exam."

That was the first they'd heard about that. They had not understood the official English report that had come through the post, and Owen had not bothered to translate it for them.

"I have no English and no nice clothes," said Jane Gruffydd.

"You don't need English," said Owen. "Everyone will be talking Welsh except those on the stage."

"Yes, go and order a coat from Ifan the Tailor," said Ifan, "and Ann Ifans will go with you for company."

And that's how it was. From his place in front of the platform Owen could see his mother and Ann Ifans sitting in the middle of the hall. He had never seen his mother wearing a coat, only a dress with perhaps a cloak over it. She looked handsome, and instead of the bonnet she had worn over the years, she had a new hat with purple flowers. Round her throat she had a white lace cravat fastened with a black brooch. Going up to get his prizes, Owen felt happier, though more nervous, because his mother was there. He was so taken up with the thought of his mother and Ann Ifans being there that he forgot about Gwen. When her turn came to get up to receive her certificate, Owen thought that the applause for her was shorter than for her class-mates. And she did not have a very good certificate either. Owen felt rather sorry for her. But she looked grand in a frock of white llama wool trimmed with braid with just a hint of colour in it.

He was glad when it was all over. He had never liked the atmosphere of the school on prize-giving day – the palm-trees on the stage, everybody dressed in their best clothes, and the snobbish atmosphere that filled the place.

When the children congregated afterwards to inspect each other's prize books, Owen went to speak to Gwen.

"That's a lovely dress you're wearing," he said, steering the conversation away from the prizes.

But this time her eyes did not light up.

"My mother and father are here," she said, "and I'll have to go to them."

"My mother is here, too," he replied. "With a friend of hers."

Gwen seemed as surprised as if she were hearing for the first time that he had a mother.

"Oh!" she said, and fled to her family.

Of all the 'Oh's' that Owen had heard in his life, that one was the most expressive. He had never heard one so full of such scornful surprise.

Later on, he was standing in the lobby, near the exit, with his mother and Ann Ifans, when he saw Gwen with her parents coming towards him on the way out. This time it was impossible for Gwen to avoid seeing him. He remembered his first prize-giving when she ignored him. This time he stood his ground and looked straight at them. The three went past without taking any notice.

"Let me see," said Ann Ifans, "wasn't that Doli Rhyd Garreg and her husband?"

"Yes," said Jane Gruffydd.

"And that was their daughter?"

"Yes," said Owen, nearly choking.

"A stuck-up little thing, isn't she?" said Ann Ifans. "She had fewer cheers than anybody."

This made them laugh, and Owen was glad of that much relief.

Because of the increasing amount of work he had to do, Owen was now forced to stay overnight in the town during the winter months, and so the three of them went to have tea in his lodging. Owen had many emotions churning about inside him: disappointment, anger, happiness. Disappointment and anger because of Gwen's behaviour; happiness because of his mother. He was mature enough to be able to forget Gwen's scorn while they were having tea, and to devote all his attentions to pleasing his mother. He was in that period of life when everything seemed to hurt him. To see his mother and Ann Ifans enjoying something so simple as a lodging-house tea and being allowed to come to a prize-giving saddened him.

"Were they teachers, Owen, those in the black capes?" asked Ann Ifans.

"Yes, they all have B.A.'s or B.Sc.'s."

"Gracious me, isn't it wonderful for them. It will be the same for you one day," she said admiringly.

"I don't know really."

"And perhaps that Doli's girl will get one too," said Jane Gruffydd, without any enthusiasm.

"No I hope not," said Ann Ifans. "I'd go so far as to say she won't get one, because the Lord knows very well who should receive a B.A."

Owen nearly choked with laughter.

"I wish I could have understood that man who was giving out the prizes," said Jane Gruffydd. "Didn't he look a proper man! Did he make a good speech Owen?"

"Yes."

"Isn't it a pity one can't understand just a little bit of English, eh, Ann Ifans?"

"I don't know really. One understands enough in this old world already. There's no knowing how much pain one avoids by not knowing English."

Jane Gruffydd and Owen laughed.

"How long is it since you were in town, Jane Gruffydd?"

"The day we weighed the pigs, but I don't count that. It's over a year since we were here just to have a look around."

"I'm sure that Owen here will take us for a trip in a closed carriage – when he begins to earn," said Ann Ifans.

"All right," said Owen, joining in the spirit of the conversation, "with my first pay packet we'll go for an outing to Anglesey."

"To Lleyn," said Jane Gruffydd.

"Yes, to Lleyn," said Owen.

And a look of sad happiness came to Jane Gruffydd's face.

"Many things will happen before that, I know," she said.

But Owen was certain that she was truly happy at that moment. It was so obvious that she had enjoyed her day. Owen looked at her when she set off, tall and dignified in her new coat, her black hair curling over her ear under her new hat, and above all showing that quiet dignity that was an inseparable part of her nature.

He was struck by the contrast between her and Gwen's mother, who was short and stout, dressed in a sealskin coat that made her look even more plump, and the veil that hid only part of her hard face.

They called for a minute at Sioned's shop. Sioned was embarrassed but did her best to be agreeable. But Elin was very glad to see them and quickly threw off her apron and cap in order to go a little along the way with them.

The crows cawed in the woods by the river, and through the trees came the colours of an Autumn sunset, fiery orange colours that riddled over the surface of the water. The hills and quarries looked dark and depressing, and there was a wintry nip in the wind.

To Owen it was a strange evening – accompanying his mother and then having to turn back without going all the way home. He felt a tenderness towards her as he turned many times to wave goodbye.

"What's the matter with you?" asked Elin.

She received no reply.

"Come in with me for a while," she said.

"No, not tonight; I'll come tomorrow night if that's all right with you."

He returned to his lodgings, went upstairs, and wept. Later, he went downstairs, and played dominoes with his landlord.

In bed that night, Owen reviewed his relationship with Gwen, and he concluded that he was a fool for ever seeing anything in her. By this time she was to him like an open book. He could see through her conceit, and he was glad that he realised this before anybody knew of their relationship. So far as he knew, nobody knew of their love affair. There had been enough of a fuss at Ffridd Felen when Sioned had done the same thing. The feeling that overcame him in bed was shame, that he had been such a fool over Gwen and so underhanded with his father and mother. Most of all he was ashamed of having been deceived, which is something no one finds bearable. It became a hateful thing in his heart and brought about a new resolution, so that he emerged from the furnace like one who had been purified. He could now leave the past behind him without regrets. It had been an experience for him, still a bitter one at present, but in the years of his life, it would occupy but a small space.

At first he had thought of sending a note to Gwen the next day, but remembering some of the things she had said about his family, and the remarks that had been made in Ffridd Felen about her mother and father he decided that a written note, although it might do Gwen a power of good and would give relief to his own feelings, might in some way hurt his family.

He saw her during the dinner-hour. She came towards him with that self-satisfied smile he had come by now to dislike so much. Quite calmly he told her.

"Since I nor my family were good enough for you yesterday, I am not good enough for you today, nor ever will be again either."

Having said this, he fled from her presence, leaving her stunned. She was going to answer him but had no opportunity. And that was the end of the first love affair of Owen Gruffydd, Ffridd Felen.

CHAPTER TEN

For the next two years in the County School, Owen concentrated all his attention on his work, and he failed to understand how he could ever have neglected it.

In Owen's last year there, Twm came to the school, having won a scholarship, and because Owen was obliged to lodge in the town, the parents thought it would be better if Twm joined him there so that Owen could keep an eye on him. Ifan and Jane Gruffydd took it for granted that some of the children could look after the others, and so take some of the responsibility off their shoulders. It could not be said that the mother and father were strict disciplinarians and the children took after them and so never carried out their duties of keeping an eye on each other. Owen had his work cut out keeping an eye on his Greek and Latin. Yet he would have to look after Twm when he shared his lodgings with him. He could not help paying attention to him. He was an exceptionally handsome boy – like his sister, Sioned, in complexion and looks, but with a more genial and open personality. When Owen passed to go to the County School, Twm had been a mere seven-year-old tot, trailing everywhere behind his sister, Bet, and so Owen did not know him as well as he knew the other children.

Every kind of work was child's play to Twm. He was a gentle child moving through life as lightly as a feather and attracting nobody's attention. Having finished his homework in a few minutes, he would then sit in a chair, whistling.

"Get on with your work," Owen would say.

"I've finished," said Twm.

"You've never done it in such a short time. Let me see."

And Twm would hand over his copy-book, still whistling

and putting his feet on the rail of the chair, holding the sides with both hands. What he said was true.

"Look here, you'll have to bring some books from the library so that you'll have something to read."

"I'd rather go out."

"Well then, go, just this once, and don't be late."

In about two hours, Twm came back, bringing with him the aroma of the chip-shop.

"Where've you been?"

"Round the docks with the other boys, and then to the chip-shop."

"Which boys?"

"The town boys in my class. Defi and Arthur."

And that's how it was all the time afterwards, without exception.

Twm enjoyed himself in the town and Owen hardly ever saw him. To Owen the lodgings were just a place to work in. He hardly ever went out. He would never come to terms with the sullen atmosphere of a town house, an atmosphere he always associated with fly-papers in September, houses with shut-in backs and no gardens, clothes lines and grimy washing. But before he had been in the town a couple of months Twm knew where to find the best chip-shop, where to buy bruised apples cheaply, every back-street and the best hiding-places in the docks. He knew every town boy in the school, and every simple or eccentric character who frequented the streets or market-place. Owen was allowed to get on with his work, and since Twm did his, he had no cause to worry.

Sometimes Twm would go to a Revivalist meeting, more out of curiosity than anything else. He managed to persuade Owen to go with him once or twice but he was not in the least bit interested in them. By this time Owen was able to maintain an exact balance between his work and outside activities. Twm went to the meetings regularly for a while and then grew tired of them. But sometimes he would tell Owen funny stories about what happened at the meetings.

Twm started going to visit Elin at her place of work and he would have supper there. Frequently he would wangle some money from her to buy his supper in the chip-shop the next night. He was more of an unknown brother to Elin than to Owen, and so she delighted in him.

He would tell her everything about his life in Ffridd Felen, and about Owen, and, yes, about Sioned too. In his wanderings about town after the shops had shut, he would often come across Sioned, dressed to kill, with some boy. From his friends he gathered that it was one of the town boys, a clerk in one of the shops. He would relish telling all this to Elin, for Sioned bridged the gap between them, and anyway, he delighted in talking and was very interested in other people's lives. When Elin had her night off on Saturday, Sioned would be working late, and afterwards would walk home or take the last coach; so Elin would hardly ever see her, and although she had begged her to call at her place of work, she never came. Because of that, Twm's account was all the more interesting.

"What kind of boy was he, Twm?" she asked.

"A bit of a lah-di-dah," said Twm. This description might not mean much to most people, but Elin understood perfectly.

"It would be far better for Sioned to go about with boys from the quarry than with such milk-sops as that. She'll find out one day that town boys are no good for her."

"Or that she is no good for town boys," said Twm.

"Don't you make a mistake," said Elin. " 'Comic Cuts' are the deepest thing some of them can understand."

When he returned to Owen, he repeated the story, adding Elin's remarks. The account would be given when they were both lying in bed because the landlady would not allow them to be extravagant with the light.

"Don't you repeat these things at home," said Owen.

"Do you think I would do such a thing?" asked Twm, feeling hurt.

"Well, I was just dropping a hint, for there has been one row there before over Sioned."

"Over what?"

And as he told his brother Sioned's history there in the dark, Owen felt that he was beginning to draw much nearer to him.

Remembering the fun his walking companions had made of boys like Sioned's young man, Owen could not resist saying, "She's a silly little fool."

"But not all the town boys are like that," said Twm.

"Even if they were like angels," said Owen, "they are different from us."

At the end of the year Owen went to the College in Bangor with a scholarship worth twenty pounds, intending to become a teacher. Only one other profession had been considered suitable for him and that was to become a preacher. But there had never been any preachers in the Ffridd Felen family, and Owen had never really felt the call. For the next three years Twm had to walk home instead of staying in the town, something that took some getting used to.

CHAPTER ELEVEN

At home, Jane and Ifan Gryffydd carried on the never-ending struggle to survive. By this time, wages in the quarry were lower than they had ever been and the cost of living was rising. Wiliam had come to the age when he paid for his own food and lodging instead of giving all his wages to his mother. This arrangement gave him more independence, but left his mother worse off. He had his keep and his washing and lots of other small services for thirty shillings a month. What Wiliam found difficult to bear was the fact that his wages were getting less as he grew older, and he could not save any money at all. This made him discontented and quarrelsome. Things were made more difficult for him and for his father by the attitude of the Steward and Little Steward towards them. The slate industry was in a precarious position because things were very slack in the building trade and because slates were being imported from abroad. But however low the wages fell, some men received more money than others by currying favour with the officials – there was many a chicken or goose on the Steward's table on a Sunday which had been in a quarryman's field the Sunday before. Because Ffridd Felen's poultry was not used in this way, they received no favours. Morus Ifan, the Little Steward, would rather do his worst than his best for the man who had once been his wife's sweetheart, and for the father and brother of one who had snatched all the prizes away from his daughter at school. In his official capacity, Morus Ifan could do no more damage than by his tongue, but through the chief Steward his influence was far-reaching.

At the beginning of the month when Buckley, the Steward, came to negotiate the price for the work, Ifan

Gruffydd could do nothing but suffer in silence. The bargain he and his partners were forced to make was a poor one, but it was useless to show disgust or to beg for a better price. If the place allotted to them to work was a good one and the rock easy to handle they could expect a low price, but since it was otherwise they could expect a much better price at the beginning of the month. But they were forced to accept this low price, and on top of it they all knew that the man who inspected the slates at the end of the month could discard more faulty ones when the market was weak.

Ifan often came home with three pounds for a month's work, sometimes four, and he considered taking home five pounds to be a very good wage. Once he took home just eighteen shillings after having worked hard for a whole month.

Until now Wiliam had had to depend on others for getting stones to work with, and he had no hope of anything better unless he could persuade some crew to take him on as a day labourer. But the day-wage man was paid so little that he would not be much better off after all. The only advantage would be that he would have a much better idea of what he was going to earn.

They were unable to repay any of the money they owed on the house. In fact, they were sometimes forced to borrow more money when it was necessary to buy a new cow after having had to sell the old one at a loss. They managed to raise enough pigs to pay the interest and the rates, but although Jane arranged to send six pigs a year to market instead of four by buying two porklings before the fatted ones had been sent away, she was not much better off. She had to pay more for pig meal, and she herself was far more tired at the end of the day.

It was true that Owen and Twm had won their schooling, but because the village, Moel Arian, was so isolated, it was an added expense to have to pay for the boys' lodgings during their last years at school. It would have been cruel to make them walk all the way home and then expect them to start on their ever-increasing amount of homework. They also needed better clothes and their books were expensive, although they received some grant towards these.

Wiliam and Elin were able to keep themselves – Wiliam failing sometimes – but Sioned never managed to do so. Her wages were not enough to keep her in food and clothes. But Jane Gruffydd managed to make enough clothes for Bet out of Sioned's old ones. When the mother wanted new clothes for herself – such as for the prize-giving – it meant getting deeper into debt.

She never saved on food. Unlike some others, she did not make a great effort to have butter to sell by putting less on the bread at home, or by mixing butter and margarine. She had one or two customers only, and these had their buttermilk free.

She worked morning, noon and night, doing the housework and most of the work with the animals. She made the children's underclothes and some of their outer garments. Before they went to the County School she would cut down Ifan and Wil's old trousers for Owen and Twm. She had little leisure for going anywhere or for reading. If she put on her spectacles to read in the evening, without fail she would fall asleep. Her husband, too, was the same, toiling and moiling in the quarry; sweating and getting wet; coming home in the winter, wet to the skin, too tired to read a newspaper. In the Spring and Summer there would be work to do on the fields every evening and Saturday afternoon.

The only respite they had would be to get up later on a Sunday morning or to go to town occasionally on a Saturday afternoon. But they never grumbled about not having holidays; they would not know what to do with them if they had frequent ones. Their lot was to be eternally troubled and anxious about paying their way in the world, to keep out of debt, and acquire those things which they needed but wondered if they could afford.

But after earthing-up the potatoes or thatching the haystack, it was a great pleasure for Ifan to lean against the wall having a leisurely smoke while admiring the work of his hands, sometimes on his own, sometimes with a friend; to see the straight rows with the newly-turned earth around the dark shoots of the potatoes; to see the side of the hay-stack smooth and solid, and enjoy the sweet smell of the hay. So it was in the quarry when he had good stones which split cleanly and easily; he would sing as the work skimmed through his hands, and then the discussion in the shed after the mid-day meal. Yes, there was still some pleasure in life.

And at nightfall, placing his foot on the low wall at the front of the house and letting his eyes rest on the sea which was red in the setting sun, a feeling of quiet satisfaction would come over him.

Wiliam was different. He had never known worse times; but he had known better ones. That was one evil that stemmed from the practice of allowing fathers to work for their sons when they first went to the quarry. It gave the youngsters an inflated idea of the quarryman's wages, and as Wiliam saw his wages going down instead of up, he blamed what was to him the obvious cause – the managers and owners. His father, on the other hand, had known better and worse times. Ifan Gruffydd knew what it was to start work at nine years old and carry loads of heavy slates on his back before his bones had begun to harden. He knew what it was to get up at four o'clock on a Saturday morning and go to the quarry by the light of a lantern and work until one o'clock in order to turn a half-day into a whole one. He knew what it was like to go into a hole and hang by a rope when he should have been in school at his lessons; the rock-face was to him what a tree is to a squirrel.

Yet, when he had been the same age as Wiliam was now, he knew what it was to earn a living wage and dream of marrying. That was before his father had been killed in the quarry. But Wiliam never had that pleasure. He developed a taste for getting about; there was a brake service to the town, and a train would take him anywhere from there.

When he was young, his father walked everywhere. That did not prevent him getting about, but it certainly helped him to save money.

A night school was started in the district at which English and Arithmetic were taught. A knowledge of Arithmetic was useful, and English allowed you to make your way in the world. It was necessary to raise the worker from his present down-trodden position. He should have a living wage. After learning a little more English than they learned in the Elementary School, the young people began to read about new ideas that were gaining ground in England and South Wales. Where their fathers (the more interested ones) had absorbed the ideas of Thomas Gee and S.R., their children grasped the ideas of Robert Blatchford and Keir Hardie.

Some of the young men began to meet in the barber's hut and they set about forming a branch of the Independent Labour Party. Wiliam was the moving spirit behind it all. Their chief task was to persuade their fellow-workers to join the Quarrymen's Union. They would not have a standard wage without that. Full of enthusiasm for the justice of their case, they felt that every quarryman would rush to join, and then there would be no difficulty in resisting any attempt to lower their wages. Their first disappointment was seeing the lack of zeal of their fellow-workers. Some were afraid of attracting the owners' animosity; others questioned what possible good could come of it; others were just not interested. Only a few were keen. Some, like Ifan Gruffydd, paid up out of a sense of loyalty. They felt that it might prove to be a good thing in the long run, in the distant future, but not in their own lifetime.

Thus it was that the present generation came to take an interest in the plight of the worker. They gathered their ideas from English books, or from the Welsh papers that echoed the English ones. The worker in Wales came to be recognised along with his counterpart in England. It was the same problem in every country, with the same enemy – Capitalism. Wiliam read everything about the matter that he could lay his hands on. And while he was wrestling with these problems nobody bothered to tell him that the very quarry in which he was working had, in the beginning, been worked by the quarrymen themselves, sharing the profits.

Their religious outlook also changed. Their grandfathers and grandmothers – the pioneers of the Nonconformist causes scattered on the hillsides – had a profound knowledge of theology. There was devotion and self-sacrifice in their religion. But the grandchildren had lost the spirit of devotion and there was little call for sacrifice. They continued to study theology, but only coldly, as something remote from their lives. They too were interested in such topics as the person of Christ, the Incarnation, Predestination and the Atonement, but only on an intellectual level rather than as concepts having a real bearing on their lives. As the conditions of their everyday lives changed, as their world seemed to be collapsing, so their attitudes towards religion changed. The change was most evident in the young. To those intent on improving the condition of the workers, a man's duty to his fellow-men was the important thing, and the Sermon on the Mount became far more important than Paul's Epistles. Their attitude towards preachers changed. The best preachers were those who preached about social justice and man's duty towards his fellow-men. The young were placated by calling Christ a Socialist. Yet this too was a matter for the intellect, not one of belief. Their interest moved from Christ the Redeemer to Christ the Example. This did not impinge upon their lives. They enjoyed a good sermon from the pulpit and a good debate in the Sunday School. But they did not have a minister with whom to agree or disagree.

Their interest in politics was partisan. The old and the middle-aged were Radicals because they believed that was best for the workers. They regarded the Tory party as the party of the Ruling Class whose sole object was to keep the worker down. Liberalism had gained ground steadily since 1868 and the quarrymen still talked about workers' freedom and his living standards. Now here was a generation of young people learning to read English and getting to know about people who were beginning to tire of Liberalism, maintaining that the great battle of the future would be between Capitalism and Labour, and that Liberalism was only another name for Capitalism. The older people were a bit suspicious of them, and the deacons and more prominent members of the chapel openly showed their disapproval because they linked the new politics with atheism. This, however, did not bring dissension into the Ffridd Felen family for they did not have deep religious or political views.

The Moel Arian branch of the Independent Labour Party did not attract a large membership, and the growth of its influence was very slow. But the few who belonged to it were very zealous. They constantly sought new members and encouraged the quarrymen to join the Union. During these years there were frequent minor strikes in the district, but these were not organised by the Union of Quarrymen. The men came out on their own initiative, very few of them receiving financial help from the Union. The men's wages continued to fall and things did not improve after a strike. It was useless trying to convince the workers that they would never be able to negotiate a minimum wage agreement without a strong Union. One of the most disappointed was Wiliam. Whenever he had the opportunity he spoke and argued on behalf of the new party. Usually he managed to get people to agree with him, but they still refused to become active members. They admired his eloquence and showed their admiration in that peculiar remark, "A bit of a case, he is, that Wiliam of Ffridd Felen." Their admiration for Lloyd George sprang from the same source.

CHAPTER TWELVE

Shortly before Owen went to College, Sioned Gruffydd, Y Fawnog, died. She had a stroke and within three days was dead without regaining consciousness. Geini and Eben had gone to live with her a few months after their marriage, for the old lady had failed to carry on working. She had absolutely refused to leave Y Fawnog although Geini had suggested that her mother should go and live in her house while she and Eben moved into Y Fawnog. With bad grace she finally agreed that Geini and her husband should come to Y Fawnog, but on her terms, not theirs. She refused to let go the reins so that once more Geini found herself working like a maid for her mother. But at least she did not have to pay rent, and, as a carpenter, Eben had a steady wage at the quarry. Old age, or some other factor, had mellowed Sioned Gruffydd's spirit. She still continued to find fault but Geini took little notice of her now. She now had Eben and there was no need for her to work so hard.

Sioned, Ffridd Felen, had too little time on a Sunday to visit her grandmother. Since she had been working in the town she did not need someone else to cover her courting adventures. When news of her grandmother's death was sent her she took little notice, and her first thought was: Will I look well in black? When she had convinced herself that she would, she found pleasure in the thought of having new clothes. She decided she would have a black dress with a white collar, and a white hat with a black ribbon. Without consulting her mother she arranged to have the dress from the shop where she worked.

Elin came to the shop to find out her intentions about going into mourning. If she could get Sioned to do the same, she wanted to defy public opinion and not go into mourning at all. But Sioned was cut to the quick by such a suggestion.

"Why?" asked Elin innocently.

"Well, think of the gossip."

"Let them talk. They won't have to pay for our clothes."

"I don't care. I've already ordered mine."

"Who's going to pay?"

"Whoever wants to. I'm certainly going to have a black outfit after my grandmother."

"Yes, I remember now; you used to be very fond of her, when it suited you."

Sioned flushed and walked off haughtily through the shop to the sewing-room. The girls, who had overheard the conversation, smiled knowingly at one another.

Elin bought some of the cheapest black material she could find and had it made up into a frock by the cheapest sempstress in the district.

The day of their mother's funeral was the first time that some of the Y Fawnog family had seen one another for many years. Betsan and Wiliam were older than Ifan. Then came Gwen, Huw, Morus, Ann, Edward and Geini. Apart from Ifan and Geini they had all left Moel Arian to live in some other parts of the country. Wiliam and Gwen lived furthest away and they were the ones most seldom seen. But, apart from Betsan, none of the others had had much to do with their mother. They came there when they heard she was ill, and found fault with Geini that she had not done this or that. They kept asking her how their mother had come to have a stroke, and wondered whether somebody had provoked her or spoken harshly to her. They hovered about the place in exactly the same way as they had done when Ifan was ill, and Geini had no opportunity to get near the bed. They sat by the bedside, giving their mother a sip of water now and again or straightening the sheet by her chin. Because Geini had to prepare food for them all, there was more work to be done looking after them than tending their mother, and not one of them offered to help wash the bedclothes.

Ifan would come there and sit by the kitchen fire, lost in thought. Now and again he would go into the bedroom, glance at his mother, and that was all. Geini felt closer to him because he acted that way. The shameless behaviour of the others drove her wild. She tried to keep her temper for she knew it would not have to be for long. But she failed once. Ann had been sitting there like a doll in the bedroom ever since ten in the morning, without moving except to have her dinner. About three in the afternoon she went to a drawer in the dresser to fetch a clean cloth to wipe the spit from her mother's mouth.

"Hold on," said Geini sharply. "Those are my towels in that drawer; mother's are the next one up."

"Oh, I didn't know you had your own things," said Ann, a bit startled.

"What do you think I had when I lived in my own house?" asked Geini.

A few nights after Sioned Gruffydd died, Eben pronounced: "A rum lot, your family."

"When your mother was alive," he continued, "none of them came here except Ifan and Betsan, but as soon as they found she was going to die they were around her like a swarm of bees and treating us like a couple of thieves."

"You're quite right," said Geini. "All of them, except Ifan, Wiliam and Betsan have been asking if she's made a will."

"Has she, I wonder?"

"I don't know. I hope she hasn't, for she'd have been sure to have given her money to those who have treated her most shabbily."

The only time the sons and daughters of Y Fawnog were gathered together was when there was a funeral. They were more strangers to one another than to their neighbours. Unlike the generation which followed them, they hardly knew one another as children even, except for those nearest to them in age. At that time, a son would be taken to a quarry and a daughter sent into service when about ten years old, and the home was nothing but a place from which to send children out into the world.

There was no depth of feeling at Sioned Gruffydd's funeral. Not one of the family thought it best not to accept offerings, for there had been no funeral there for thirty-five years. It was agreed that Wiliam, as the oldest son, should receive the offerings, and he sat on the settle by the fire with a round table before him on which was spread a large, white black-bordered handkerchief to receive the gifts. On his marriage he had left home and gone to live in Pont-y-Braich, and so only the old and middle-aged knew him. Sioned Gruffydd's other children and her children-in-law sat on chairs arranged against the kitchen walls. Not one of her brothers or sisters was alive. The grandchildren stood outside by the door inspecting each other's clothes, some of them seeing their cousins for the very first time.

The kitchen was dark and close. The curtains there and in the bedroom did not quite reach the bottom of the windows and a little light percolated through these gaps and through the open door. Those who faced the inner door could not see a beam of light falling on the coffin in the bedroom. All the daughters wore black clothes and they had crepe on their hats. Gwen had some crepe on her coat and skirt as well. The scent of pinewood drifted from the bedroom, mingling with the smell of black kid-gloves from the kitchen. Every time someone entered the room, Gwen turned her head, and if she did not recognise them, she asked Geini in a loud voice to identify them: Geini had to tell her to be quiet. Betsan had for some time been trying to produce the same effect on Gwen by darting furious glances at her. The people came in one by one, placing their sixpences on the table. If they were Wiliam's contemporaries, they would say,

"How are you, lad, after such a long time?"

The others would turn from the table and return to mingle with the crowd outside. Occasionally, an unexpected silence would descend when nobody entered, and in this silence would be heard the lazy sound of the big kettle singing gently on the hearth, and reflected from it was a ray of light that had come down through the chimney. So familiar was the sound of the kettle to Geini that momentarily she thought she was preparing tea and the funeral was only a dream. Then the last group of people entered, and in the silence that followed came the voice of the preacher giving out the hymn. At the graveside, Ifan was the only one who cried. Owen stared at him for that was the only time he had seen his father crying.

Shortly before the funeral the schoolmaster had called at Ffridd Felen to say that Sioned Gruffydd had made a will, and he had it in his possession for he had drawn it up for her. She had told him not to say a word about it until the day of the funeral, and because all the family was together, he proposed to read the will after tea. So, the schoolmaster had to come and have tea with them, and for most of them it was without doubt the most unpleasant meal they had had for years.

There, at the table after the tea-things had been removed, was read the last will and testament of Sioned Gruffydd. During tea the schoolmaster had looked anxious for he knew that the content of the will would please none of them. The old woman had left all her money to her grand-daughter, Sioned of Ffridd Felen. The will was dated October 12th, 1899 – shortly after Geini was married. That moment was a dreadful one for all those present, including the schoolmaster, but nobody showed his feelings whilst he was there. Geini went pale, and Ifan trembled. They were the two most deeply hurt by the news. The schoolmaster rose to go, and Wiliam said he would have to catch his train.

"Wait a minute," said Wiliam, with beads of sweat on his

forehead. "Is there anything there about the furniture and the farm implements, Mr Evans?"

"No, nothing at all. Only about the money she had in the bank."

"Are you sure that's the last will my mother made?"

"Yes, so far as I know. Well, good afternoon,"and the schoolmaster fled.

"Sit down a minute," said Ifan to Wiliam.

"Why should I stay? It would be far better for me to catch my train."

"Not at all. You heard what the schoolmaster said about the furniture."

"I don't care about that."

"But the others do."

"Yes," said Ann, the feathers in her hat bristling. "We must watch that they don't go to the same place as the money."

She fixed her eyes on Ifan. And except for Wiliam, Betsan and Geini the others followed her example.

"It's obvious that someone was getting his children to hang on mother's sleeve to get money to send his children through school," said Gwen.

Some idea of what she was thinking dawned on Ifan, and seeing the self-righteous, wounded looks on the faces of most of his family, all the injustices of a lifetime that had gathered in his breast broke loose.

"See here," he said, his voice trembling. "If you think I'm going to get a penny piece of this money from my daughter Sioned, you are all very much mistaken. She is over twenty-one and can do what she likes with it, and I'm pretty sure that neither I nor anybody else in my family will see a penny of it. And even if I got the money it would only be going where it should have gone in the first place. It's my money. I earned it after father died, and I was a big enough fool to give it all, nearly every penny of it, to mother. There I was, working like a navvy in this place, and that at a time when some of you were able to swagger about town every Saturday night, thinking that you'd done your duty by giving a little something for your food, and spending the rest on clothes and beer. But I would prefer Geini to have the money for she did most for mother in her later years when everybody else was keeping his distance."

"Quite true," said Betsan.

Ifan wiped the sweat from his brow with his white handkerchief. That was the longest speech he had made in his life.

Gwen, Huw, Edward, Ann and Morus sniffed their disapproval.

Wiliam placed his umbrella on the chair indicating that he was prepared to miss his train and wait for the next one.

"There's no mention of the furniture and the stock?" he asked.

"No," said Ifan.

"It's a wonder that he didn't point that out to her, and he a schoolmaster" said Edward.

"He probably realised they would have gone to the same place," said Betsan.

"You're probably right," said Ifan.

"Well, I propose," said Betsan, "that Geini gets all the furniture and everything here including the two cows, the two pigs, the haystack and such-like. I would suggest that Ifan should have half of them if I knew that he wouldn't have any of the money from Sioned, but I'm sure she'll give some of it to her own father and mother."

The others laughed spitefully.

"Why should Geini have more than the rest of us?" asked Morus.

"Because she's earned it by staying at home to look after mother," said Ifan, "and none of you can say the same."

"No, she certainly mustn't," said Gwen. "I propose that everything be sold and the proceeds shared equally among us all."

"And everyone will get a paltry six pounds each," said Betsan.

"Some of us will be glad of even that much," said Morus, the poorest and most shiftless of them all. His wife was as extravagant as he: he was one of those who eat the bread the day it is baked.

"Look here, Wiliam," said Ifan. "You're the eldest. You take things in hand. There are two proposals already. I want to go home."

"Yes, I'm sure, to give your daughters the good news," said Owen.

"Well," said Geini, who had been struck dumb until now, "I certainly don't want to take anything without everybody agreeing, and since that's the legal position then it's best that everything should be sold and the money shared."

And that is how it was settled.

In the Ffridd Felen there was a tea-party. Jane Gruffydd had gone straight home from the cemetery, and out of consideration for Geini she had taken all the children of the family home with her to have tea. The children enjoyed themselves and their admiration for their Aunt Jane was obvious. While Elin and her mother sat by the fire having a chat before Elin would have to return to the town, the children played in the fields, in the yard, and in every hole and corner of the cowshed and the outhouses. They got on famously together and hoped to see more of each other in the future. The strangers thought that Ffridd Felen was a marvellous place. Upstairs, admiring herself in the mirror was Sioned.

Ifan Gruffydd arrived home, and seeing the children so happy together another lump came to his throat. He disliked having to break up their happy companionship and tell them to seek their parents in Y Fawnog.

This day had been the strangest in Ifan Gruffydd's life since his father died. But even that one had been a happy one compared with this.

That day he had felt but one kind of emotion, of grief and pity; grief for his father, that quiet, kind, man who had walked with him to the quarry ever since he had started working, and a feeling of pity for his mother left a widow with such a burden on her; and a feeling too of the cruelty of fate that could strike a man down in his prime, denying him the comfort he had so richly earned at the end of his life.

Today it was different. His mother had been allowed to live to old age. In her last years she had been most ungrateful to those of her children who had been good to her, and this Ifan found difficult to understand. She had not been like that when she was bringing up her children. Listening to her complaining before she died, her younger days had come to life in his memory – those days when she had worked from morning to night. He remembered that she, just as much as his father, had been responsible for transforming Y Fawnog from a barren mountainside into quite a productive little farm. The other day, taking slate slabs to her grave and seeing his father's headstone sunk into the ground, he had felt how strange it was to place side-by-side the bodies of two people who had lived together at one time and had then been apart such a long time. His father's death was in the memory alone, and not in the feelings. Emotions which had burned and hurt at one time had cooled and hardened. He was saddened by the thought of the great changes that must inevitably come in men's lives. He had wanted to stand at his mother's grave today, his mind full of kind thoughts about her, and yet those thoughts would eventually become colder just like less kindly thoughts. But after the reading of the will he felt that every sad thought he had had during the week had been in vain.

And yet, as he heard the happy shouts of his own children as well as those of his nephews and nieces as he opened the gate to the yard outside his home, the same lump came to his throat as had been there at his mother's graveside.

CHAPTER THIRTEEN

Sioned appeared completely unmoved when the news of the money was broken to her, and she gave no indication that she might give some of it to her family. In the shop she was the same, and the other girls who worked there did not know that she had come into money. She went on with her work more independently than ever, if that was possible. The only person to whom she revealed any sign of pleasure was Bertie Ellis, her latest boy-friend. That first evening she went to tell him, and disclosed her true happiness.

"And now," she said, "there is nothing to stop us marrying."

"Well, no, as far as I can see."

"As far as I can see what?"

"Well, nothing, I was just wondering."

"Wondering about what?"

"Whether we could live on a guinea a week."

"You are not going to earn just a guinea forever. You'll get a rise sometime, I hope."

"Well, perhaps, though I doubt it. Trade is a bit slack nowadays."

"Oh, well, we'll manage somehow; at least we'll be able to buy furniture with this money."

"I don't like the thought of taking your money. A pity I couldn't win that crossword competition, isn't it?"

"You'll never win it. Better by far if you kept your sixpences."

"You haven't a high opinion of my brains."

"Not for solving crossword puzzles, anyway."

When the hundred-and-twenty pounds that Sioned had after her grandmother was ready to be handed over to her, her father and mother had a talk with her one Sunday. They disliked such conversations with any member of the family, but more so with Sioned. When a snail puts out its horns from its shell there's a chance of doing something about it, but when it insists on staying inside its shell...

"Now then, Sioned," said her father. "What are you going to do with the money besides keeping it in the bank?"

This took the wind from her sails for a moment. Lately, she had been allowed to manage her own affairs to such an extent that she did.not expect any interference now.

"I don't know," she said, twisting her handkerchief.

"Don't you think you might like to give some of it to help us to fnish paying for the boy's schooling?"

Sioned did not reply.

"And," said the mother, "in a manner of speaking, it's your father's money."

"How's that?" she asked, and her voice betrayed her fear that her good luck might desert her.

"Well," said her father, "it isn't easy to explain, but my mother saved that money when I was at home before I was married. There would have been more if my mother had not had to spend some of it to keep herself of course."

"The money is mine according to the will, isn't it?"

"Yes, but we thought you might like to help your mother and father a bit."

"Why don't the boys help the same way as you did?"

"It's not the same thing, as you know full well. Since the boys have won scholarships it's right they they should have some education."

"Well, I'm not going to pay for it. I'm going to get married."

Neither of the parents was surprised to hear this for they were quite prepared for any thunderbolt coming from the direction of their daughter Sioned, who was so different from the others.

Overcome by sadness, the two remained silent.

When she was able to speak, the mother said, "Who is the

young man, if I'm not asking too much?"

"Someone from the town."

"What's his job?"

"A clerk."

"With whom?"

"With Davies and Johnson."

"Does he earn a reasonable salary?"

"I can't say really."

"Oh," said the father, "you'd prefer to give a hundred and twenty pounds to a stranger rather than your own family?"

"I'm not giving them."

"You be careful, my girl, or you won't have it for long. It's rather remarkable that you should be marrying now, so soon after getting the money."

In the cowshed, sitting on a handkerchief spread on the manger wall, Owen and Twm were discussing the situation. Owen had finished in the County School, but he did not yet know his examination results so the question of going to College was still undecided. Deep inside him he knew he would go. His mother and father would be sure to get the money somehow, but that was the question – how to get it? A good deal of money was needed if he was to live in a town for three years. Twm had only just started his education, and was not quite old enough to understand the complexities of life, but he was old enough to realise that a lot of money would be needed if he was to remain in school, and he well knew what a small wage his father had.

"And to think," said Owen, "that it was Sioned who had the money; if only Elin or Wiliam or you or me had been given it. But Sioned!"

"Yes," said Twm, "it'll go like a hot knife through butter. She'll be swanking all over the place."

"Swanking?"

"Cutting a dash."

"Or she'll marry that young man you saw her with."

At this, Bet came by and, picking up a milking-stool from the runnel and placing it directly in front of the two boys, she sat down and stared at them. Bet had a habit of doing this to people she did not see very often – staring at them as if she could not believe that there were such people in the world.

"Sioned is going to get married," was her first piece of news.

"Go on; you've been listening in the hayloft."

"No indeed; I've been listening in the house."

Bet had gone into the house and had overheard the tail-end of the conversation between Sioned and her parents.

"She was telling mother and father just now," said Bet.

"Well, that clinches it," said Twm, "we shan't see any of that money."

Wiliam came from somewhere.

"Hullo Wil; have you heard the news?" shouted Twm. "Sioned is going to marry one of the toffee-noses."

"Yes, I know," he said curtly. "She'd rather share her money with strangers."

"What would you do if you had been left the money?" asked Owen.

"I'd open my own quarry."

"And share the money between the workers, like a true Socialist," said Owen.

Wiliam went out, hurt. His only ambition these days was to escape the Steward's clutches.

"Now then," said Owen to Bet, "what are the chances of your winning a scholarship?"

"None," said Bet. "I can't do sums."

Owen felt relieved at this. For one more member of the family to win a scholarship would be to tempt Providence too much.

Sioned's impending marriage caused a good deal of pain in Ffridd Felen. Sometimes Jane Gruffydd felt like telling her to go and never come back again. But once she'd said this there would be no end to the gossip in the district, and some of her in-laws would, despite their animosity towards Sioned, make out that things were much worse than they really were. The only comfort the mother derived from the whole affair was being able to prove to those members of the family who were against Ifan that it was not the household of Ffridd Felen who had received the substance of Sioned Gruffydd's will. Some of them came to offer sympathy. Their commiseration was accepted at its face value, and they went away biting their lips and wondering how Jane Gruffydd was able to accept everything so calmly.

On one thing Ifan and Jane Gruffydd were adamant; the wedding was not to take place in Moel Arian.

Throughout those Summer holidays this pain hung over the Ffridd Felen and, as Owen and Twm were at home all the time, they felt the brunt of it. Owen was almost tempted to go and look for work over the holidays, and if such work was available, he would have taken it. He and Twm ate as much as four people. They wore-out many pairs of trousers and boots. But they helped as much as possible; carrying water, churning the milk, fetching heather ready for the haystack, cleaning-out the cowshed and pigsty, but there was plenty of time left over, and even more time for their mother to worry.

Sioned was married in town in a light grey dress with yards of white tulle around her neck, and Bertie wore a silk hat and tail-coat. The Ffridd Felen family was represented by Owen and Elin, and the two were glad that the wedding was in the town – they thought of Bertie and his silk hat in Moel Arian! The more he looked at him, the more Owen was reminded of Twm's description of him – a 'la-di-dah'. He was one of those people whose minds would never develop, and whose skin would remain eternally young-looking. But they both had to confess that Sioned looked very beautiful.

And so, Sioned's ambition to live in the town was fulfilled, in a house with a parlour with a wooden floor – not a best kitchen with a tiled floor like the one at Ffridd Felen; with venetian blinds and a plush sofa with cushions instead of a horsehair one with anti-macassars.

After about a fortnight Sioned and Bertie came up from town on a Sunday afternoon. They had tea in the best kitchen, and the best crockery was on the table. Everybody was unnatural and ill-at-ease; the menfolk were punctual and walked aimlessly about, as people do before an important occasion like a preaching festival or a funeral. Bet ran about in her new shoes, buttoned high with wide toes, the stiff frills of her white apron flared out over the shoulders of the black-and-white dress she had had after her grandmother. Her hair, which had been arranged into a dozen plaits the night before, stood out as stiff as a crinoline, some of it tied above her ears with a white ribbon. She followed the boys every-where, clapping her hands behind her back and in front of her body. Jane Gruffydd was the most natural of them all for she was the busiest, putting a final sprinkling of fine white sugar over the cake and wiping dust from the tea-cups.

When the click of the yard-gate was heard, everybody felt apprehensive except Bet who, in her own particular manner, dashed out to meet them with an admiring look. For her, a ten-year-old child, there really was something to admire, the white tulle frothing around Sioned's face, and Bertie in his silk hat and tail-coat. Owen's heart sank; he could see the married couple going up the chapel aisle that evening, with the other members of the Ffridd Felen family in front and behind them like a retinue, with the eyes of all the people in the chapel boring through their clothes and flesh into the marrow of their bones.

Tea-time passed without much conversation or eating. Everybody did his best, but the only one who did not feel uncomfortable was Bet. She kept on asking for more apple tart until Twm had to kick her under the table, and she gave him an innocent look implying that her sister's husband, at any rate, did not wish to stop her eating.

At one point they thought that they had struck on one topic of conversation that might be discussed generally.

"You have a nice view from here," said Bertie, who was sitting opposite the window.

"Yes," said Ifan Gruffydd, "you won't often see a view like this with plenty of mountain and sea."

"You can see Ireland on a very clear day," said Owen.

But Bertie's conversation had dried up.

"Will you have a cigarette?" he said to his father-in-law.

"No, thank you, I prefer a pipe."

"Wiliam?"

"No, no thanks."

He would have liked one, but he did not wish to show his brother-in-law that he was not used to smoking cigarettes.

As the time for chapel drew near Owen's heart sank. He felt like putting his fingers down his throat to make himself sick, or anything as an excuse for staying at home.

And then the crucial question came from his father.

"What do you two want to do? Are you coming to the chapel?"

Sioned looked at Bertie and he at her.

"No, not tonight," he said. "We'll have to start back almost immediately." Owen could have hugged him in gratitude. Ifan did not know whether his son-in-law was raised or lowered in his estimation by refusing to come to the chapel.

Owen and his mother stayed at home with the young couple, and they went round the premises looking at the animals, but Bertie was not interested in them.

"Have you ever tried doing anagrams?" he asked Owen.

For once Owen had to confess ignorance: "I don't know what anagrams are."

"Like this," said Bertie, taking a red book from his pocket. "Here's a word, and you have to make two or three words to describe it with the same letters as those in the word itself. With your brains you should be able to make up some good ones. I know a chap in town who has won £300 for one."

"Come on," said Sioned, "or we'll never get home."

"Won't you have something before you go?" asked Jane Gruffydd.

"No, we'll go now before they come out of chapel," said Sioned.

That afternoon, Sioned learnt the simple fact that country people are not always taken in by grandeur.

After they had gone, Owen said to his mother, "Oh, bring me something to eat, I'm nearly starving."

"Really, you should have eaten more at tea-time. I don't know how such a harmless little creature as that could have such an effect on your appetites!"

CHAPTER FOURTEEN

Towards the middle of the following September, Jane Gruffydd was in town buying a trunk for Owen to take with him to College. He had won a scholarship worth twenty pounds and this, along with a grant from the Teachers' Training Department, would enable him to pay his College expenses, buy his books and pay his academic fees.

She walked about the shops slowly and listlessly. It was one of those warm September days when the heat and the haze of the afternoon is followed by a cold, clear moonlit night. Everywhere, people bustled about, their summer clothes having a new lease of life after some rainy weeks in Autumn. The shop windows, and their entrances, were laden with ripe fruit, and there was the buzz of countless wasps hovering over everywhere. The windows were tarnished by insect dirt.

Jane had walked to the town in the heat of noon. Her face dripped with sweat and her hair looked as if it had been dragged out of the river. She had only one coat for summer and winter. Yet she felt very happy. It was a joy to her that Owen had won a scholarship, and as Ann Ifans had told her, she ought to be proud of her son.

She went into the ironmonger's shop and welcomed its coolness after the heat of the street.

"These are very popular nowadays," said the man, pointing to some wooden trunks after she had told him what she wanted.

"How much is that one?"

"Thirty shillings."

Jane trembled in surprise.

"No, I'll have to get something cheaper than that."

"Well, there's a lot of go on these," and he showed her some big wicker-work baskets with large lids. She thought one of these would do so long as he put his books in a sugar-box.

Jane was glad that the basket cost less than she expected. But shirts and such things cost more and the pound that she had saved from the monthly wage went like water through a sieve. She wondered whether there would ever come a time when she would come to town with more money than she needed to buy things. Yes, that time would surely come. Owen would come to earn, and Twm: they would have good wages, and she would be able to repay her debts and then buy a few luxuries. She bought some plums to take home; these were luxuries.

She went to Sioned's house, where her daughter was glad to see her and hurried to make a cup of tea. Her flushed face turned into a yellow pallor, and Sioned could not help noticing this.

"Are you ill, Mam?"

"No, it's just that I've hurried through the heat."

"It was far too hot for you to walk. Why didn't you take the brake?"

"I'm going to go back in it, but I must nip along to see Elin for a minute. It's very expensive to take the brake both ways. Oh, this tea is good."

"Do you feel better now?"

"Yes, I feel much more myself."

"You're wearing a very heavy coat."

"Yes, but it will have to do; soon it will be winter again."

"Come and see the house."

The mother had to admire the plush chairs, the stained-walnut furniture and the new-fashioned bed with all its brass knobs.

"I'll go as far as Nel's place with you," said Sioned, "if you must go now."

Later on, in the kitchen of Elin's place, Jane Gruffydd sat facing the window and listening intently for the sound of the brake, which was due any minute. She would forget the time when talking to Elin.

"Didn't Sioned offer you anything?"

"No, but she was very agreeable, and I had a nice cup of tea."

"She couldn't do less, I hope."

'Well, I've seen her do less. It's good to see her no longer frowning and able to treat one like another human being."

"Huh, she could easily give you some of that hundred and twenty pounds, since you've got so many bills to pay just now."

"I'd rather she didn't."

The familiar sound of horses' hooves was heard, and then a crunching as the brake came to a halt.

Elin waved to her mother and bit her lip to stop herself crying. Years, of service in the town had not weaned her from Ffridd Felen.

Jane sat in the brake, with Owen's basket tied to the side, swaying as the brake moved. To her, the basket was a sign that the family was really breaking up. Although Elin and Sioned were in the town and the boys were at school, she did not feel that they had left town, because they were so near. She could not take her eyes off the basket, which seemed to her like a symbol of some cruel fate. Usually, in the middle of the week, the brake was filled with women and there was a greater tendency to talk.

"When is Owen starting at the college?" asked one.

"In three weeks."

"You'll find it odd without him."

"Yes, for a while, I'm sure."

"That's the way it is, once they begin to go."

"Yes, and there's precious little to keep the boys here."

"True, and it's very difficult for some of the older ones too. But your boys will get good situations."

"I don't know. So many things can happen. It costs

enough to set them up anyway."

A breeze was blowing by this time and the haze was lifting from the face of the sea. The corn was standing in stooks in the fields or was being carried in on wagons. The sea lay beside them now and it looked somehow different from how it looked from Ffridd Felen. There were dark shadows on it and it had a deeper colour. Jane turned her head to look at Moel Arian, and it too looked different as the windows of the rectangular farmhouses winked gold in the sun. The quiet of September was on the face of the earth with only a hint of changing colour on the trees. Under this influence, a deep calm came over Jane as the horses pulled slowly up the hill, their hooves striking hard against the road and steam rising from their backs. The next generation that came to travel this road in motor-cars would not experience this satisfaction of the spirit; neither would they see wonderful views over the tops of hedges.

Every member of the family of Ffridd Felen was as a little child when mother went to town, and they all rushed to her basket when she returned.

There was nothing for her to do when she arrived home. The boys had lifted enough potatoes for the quarryman's supper, and they had milked the cows two hours earlier than usual so that she would not have to do it when she arrived home.

"My dear boys," she said, "their udders will be bursting tomorrow, and I'll have to get up at the crack of dawn to milk them."

CHAPTER FIFTEEN

On a Monday morning in December, 1908, it was as busy in the Ffridd Felen kitchen as if it were mid-day, or even busier. It was four o'clock in the morning, and breakfast-time for Wiliam and his parents. Twm and Bet sat by the fire under the big chimney having had a cup of tea on the hob; and if it were not for the occasion, Twm and Bet would have been beside themselves with excitement. Nothing gave Bet greater pleasure than to get up at some unearthly hour and have breakfast by the fire, having pulled her frock over her nightdress. Although it was only four in the morning, there was a bright fire in the grate and a warm atmosphere in the kitchen. Jane Gruffydd had been on her feet since half past two although Wiliam's pack had been prepared the night before. In Ffridd Felen, the mother of the family was out of bed first, and consequently the kitchen never had that cold aspect that belongs when the fire has just been lit.

Wiliam was going to south Wales and was catching the mail train from Bron Llech station.

"Remember to hold your clothes in front of the fire, Wiliam. They are well aired, but you'd better show them to the fire. And watch that you don't get a damp bed, and I hope you'll get good lodgings with someone from these parts."

"There are plenty of people there from these parts, they say, but Jac says it would be better if I went to stay with southerners; it would be better in the long run."

"Very likely," said his father drily, "those wouldn't be writing to anybody from these parts."

"And remember to write to say that you've arrived. Is that postcard in your pocket?"

"Yes."

By this time, Wiliam was sitting on the armchair with his feet on the fender, tying his bootlaces. He was keeping his head down so that no one could see he was close to tears. This was the first time he was going to spend the night away from home.

"I hope you'll have company," said his mother, "and that you won't catch cold."

The mother continued to talk for the same reason that Wiliam kept his head down.

And now William was putting on his overcoat; he put his bowler hat on his head and wrapped a big scarf twice round his neck. He picked up the big basket which had been sitting like Fate on the kitchen table since the previous evening, the same basket that had danced on the side of the brake four years earlier and had seen Owen's setting off for College.

"Well," said Wiliam, "goodbye, all," and without looking at anybody, he followed his father into the darkness. The mother fetched a lamp to light their way, but a gust of wind sent a tongue of flame up the glass. She ran back to put the lamp on the table and when she went outside again she could only see two dark shapes by the gate, and one shouting, "Did you find it?" as they groped for the catch on the gate. The darkness absorbed them.

She shut the door and went to sit by the fire where Twm and Bet were staring dreamily into the flames. A heavy silence fell on the kitchen.

"Well," said Jane Gruffydd, "it wouldn't do for me to doze off. Go to bed, Bet, and you, Twm. It's far too early for you to be up before school."

And she set about clearing the table and cleaning the boots. This was the morning she had been dreading for weeks. Ever since Wiliam had said defiantly that he would not be a beggar in the quarry any more and that he was going South, there had been a burden on her heart.

All the other children were comparatively near; but the

South – it was the other side of the world! And she had always taken for granted, somehow, that Wiliam would never leave home except to get married. And now he was gone to the other end of the world, and to work that was completely different. Life was very hard. But really she did not know which was harder to bear, seeing Wiliam leaving home like this or seeing him arrive home every evening, miserable and dispirited. Wages in the valley had reached rock bottom.

Soon Ifan Gruffydd returned home having had the company of the postman on the way up. Now he had to set off on the three-mile walk to work, and alone this day.

In the train Wiliam sat with his hand under his chin. The train went past houses and he could see lights flickering in their windows. He could imagine the wife cutting bread-and-butter, and filling the food-tin and tea-bottle. The man would be discarding the dirty handkerchief from his pocket and taking up a clean one. His boots would be warming on the fender, black for today, a Monday, and made supple by grease that had not dryed out yet in the lace-holes, and sweating in the heat of the fire. The man would put his head out of the door and call out, "No, it isn't raining. I won't take a sack today." He'd throw an old coat over his shoulders, fastening it with a safety-pin.

"Oh God!" groaned Wiliam, "Why couldn't I be setting off in the same way?"

And then his hatred of the quarry came back to him. He pictured it, black on the mountainside with a grey cap of cloud on its head, like an old witch making fun of him, and he groping his way towards it on a dark morning like this, and no work for him to start on when he arrived there in the cold of the morning, only going about with his hands in his pockets, begging. That's what it was, and nothing else. Going from one table to the next and standing there like a mute. One or two would give him an unsplit stone to work with, but most would refuse. Being courteously refused by some because of the real shortage of stones, being coldly refused by others, and being hypocritically refused by some of the meaner ones. There was nothing better than being a casual worker for getting to know people.

There was that old Wil Evans (Wiliam seethed to think of him now) refusing in his cunning way to give him a stone one summer afternoon. Dead on knocking-off time that afternoon, a load of stones from the quarry face came for Wil and Wiliam decided to ask him first thing the following morning. That night in bed he had some kind of intuition and he went to work half an hour earlier than usual. As he expected, who should be there already but old Wil Evans, having split a large number of stones and with a big pile of untrimmed slates on his bench. He could not stomach asking him for a stone then, but he made sure that everybody in the quarry knew about it.

And then at the end of the month how difficult it was to put up with the frowns of the overseer if he had not split enough slates, and then to have to beg for more stones.

He thought of his father having agreed to terms at the beginning of the month, and very often they were very bad terms, and not knowing whether he would be paid for his labour at the end of the month. A quarryman's wage was like a lucky dip. And then there was the rash of minor strikes which had broken out in the last few years. Not a halfpenny coming in from anywhere and everybody eating more than his ration through being home all day. His mother had to pluck up courage to face the shopkeeper, and the shopkeeper had to be patient.

In his opinion the quarrymen were blind not to see the advantages of joining the Union and fighting for a minimum wage and standard working agreements. Many more had joined recently, but not enough.

What was the point of kicking up a fuss and coming out on strike if they did not have the strength of the Union behind them? Well, perhaps they were content to have their feet in chains.

Those were Wiliam's thoughts as the train moved slowly along, puffing like a man going up a steep hill. Sometimes it would stop at a dreary little station, quiet as the grave, the silence punctuated only by the snorts of steam from the engine. In the darkness the porter would hold his lamp aloft and its beams would form a circle of light in the morning mist. Then he would turn the lamp again and the train would slowly pull away, leaving the porter and his lamp buried in the darkness. Soon Wiliam became tired of thinking and fell asleep.

Once more during the journey the scenes at the quarry came alive into his mind. He was nearing the end of his journey and night was drawing in again. He could see the men in the shed, their caps pulled down over their eyes, cold and miserable, waiting by the doors of the shed for the hooter to sound. Like grey rats in their holes they would peer around the doorposts. Then, when the hooter blew, they rushed headlong like a pack of hounds down the tramline towards the mountain. He remembered those faces now, hard-looking but hiding much geniality. They managed to laugh when things were at their blackest and made fun even of low wages. Many of them were dying of consumption.

Once more, thinking about the quarry, he began to boil with indignation. He would like to kill Morus Ifan, the Little Steward. He knew he had something personal against his father and would like to sack him, but his father could control his temper, something Wiliam could never do. He relived the scene when he was given notice. He had gone to see Buckley, the Steward, to ask for something better than casual labour, but he was not to be found, so he asked Morus Ifan instead. He remembered the look of contempt on his face. That was enough, but when he began reproaching him for his association with the Labour Party and his work for the Union, Wiliam could not restrain himself and went for his throat. It was lucky for the Little Steward that somebody happened to come by at that moment. Hatred for him welled up inside, and he faced the coal-pit ahead of him with strength and determination.

CHAPTER SIXTEEN

The day that Wiliam went away was a very strange one at Ffridd Felen. The mother felt that she did not have the heart to do the washing or anything else. In the afternoon she went up to Twnt i'r Mynydd.

"I was thinking of you," said Ann Ifans, "and thought of coming down this evening. I could have come down this morning but there was something wrong with this cow here."

"You don't say."

"It's nothing much. She drank too much water when she was let out for a minute yesterday, and came in shivering with her hair standing on end."

"It's one trouble after another. In this world it's not enough just to be poor..."

"No, indeed. It's a hard world."

"I can't remember times as bad as these, and yet mother says that it was worse when she was young."

"That's what my mother says, too. But things won't stay so bad; they'll improve with time."

"I'm sure they won't," said Ann Ifans in that mournful tone of voice which is peculiar to people of a happy disposition. "But how was Wiliam when he set off?"

"I think he was on the point of breaking down, and struggling to keep control of himself."

"His father will see it strange in the quarry without him."

"Yes, dreadfully."

"But you'll find that Wiliam will be all right once he's arrived and starting to earn money. They tell me there's good money to be earned down there in the South."

"I hope so, indeed, but there are so many killed in those coal-pits."

"There are plenty killed here in the quarries, so far as that goes, and many dying from consumption."

"Yes, that's true enough."

"Then there are those shops in town. I don't know who'd place his dog there, let alone a child."

"Yes, the pay is very small."

"I should say it's small; just think of our John, getting only fifteen shillings a week, standing behind the counter from dawn to dusk, and that old man walking about the shop peering into every corner. If he could buy more eyes to put in his head, he would do so, he's so frightened of somebody stealing something from him."

Jane Gruffydd laughed.

"How's Owen?"

"Very well. I had a letter from him this morning and he likes the place very much."

"It's good that someone's happy."

"But remember, his pay is not half enough considering what his education cost us."

"I don't suppose it is."

"He's paying ten shillings a week for lodgings, and buying his own food."

"Heaven help us!"

"Yes, and the lad is trying to send a little money home every month."

"Fair play to him. He's a good lad, is Owen."

"Yes," said Jane Gruffydd, "not one of them has given me so much pain as Sioned, you know."

"How is she, and her husband and the little boy?"

"Oh, they're all right. The baby's a lovely little thing, but I can't make anything of her husband. I don't believe he has a grain of sense in him. But Sioned keeps everything to herself. It would have been far more just if we, or Geini, had received Ifan's mother's money."

"Didn't Sioned give you any?"

"Not a penny piece. How useful it would be now! There's Twm again, going to college shortly."

And thus the two women talked about their circumstances, understanding little of the underlying causes yet being extremely sensitive to their effects. They could do nothing about it but carry on from day to day hoping that things would improve. Having a chat with a neighbour somehow lightened the mental burden.

Ifan Gruffydd arrived home fully ten minutes later than usual that night. As soon as he had eaten he fell asleep in the armchair. His wife noticed the dark rings under his eyes and saw his hard, toil-worn hands.

One thing that changes when the children have left home is the importance of the postman. When the family are all together at home, receiving a letter is something remarkable. But once the children have begun to go away, the postman comes closer to the family, and becomes a person of significance.

And yet, although she kept a sharp look-out while bending over the wash-pan the following morning, no word came. In Jane Gruffydd's imagination, the South was three times more distant than in reality. And yet she expected a letter in quick time.

The card arrived on the Wednesday morning, and when Wiliam mentioned in it that he had company on the journey, the mother felt that it had taken place a month ago. Within a few days a letter arrived from him, brief and brusque in style, revealing nothing of his true feelings. He had got a job and found a lodging with some very kind southerners. There was no mention of his home-sickness, nor of his shyness when he was given a tub to wash in front of the fire, nor of the dark-eyed daughter of the house. The nearest hint of his longing for home was a postscript mentioning the loaf of bread and the butter his mother had put in his pack, which was very good.

The duty of writing a letter that Sunday was placed on Twm. He was a first-class letter-writer, but so well did his letters convey the atmosphere of home that they made the recipient homesick.

CHAPTER SEVENTEEN

Twm was in his last two years at the County School and because he was a good student, he was lodging in the town. At first he went to stay with his sister, Sioned. She appeared anxious to have him although the parents felt it would be better if he went to stay with strangers. He took most of his food down with him each week, bought his own dinner in town, and paid his sister three shillings a week. After a while he began to run out of bread, butter, bacon and eggs before the end of the week; he knew this should not happen because it was easy to check his provisions, eggs especially.

One week he had run out of bread, eggs and bacon by Thursday morning, and he had to buy a loaf out of his pocket-money. This had happened once before, but at that time he had more money. This time he could only afford to buy this one loaf of bread. On Friday morning at breakfast, Sioned said to him:

"You've eaten a great deal this week. Never mind, you'd better have some of my butter." She handed him a pat of some insipid shop butter.

Twm was angry. "You and your shop butter. Keep your trash. I'm not the one who has eaten the pound I brought from home on Friday morning, and I'm not the one who has eaten the eggs either, I've only had four of them."

Sioned collapsed into a chair and cried, while Bertie looked at Twm as if he had murdered his sister.

"Shame on you, upsetting Jane like that. Are you accusing your sister of stealing your food?" he said in his effeminate voice.

"No," said Twm, drawing himself up to his full height, and looking down on his brother-in-law. "I know she has only borrowed them because you don't give her enough."

At this, Sioned sobbed and Eric, the child, came down-stairs, crying, Bertie tried to look dignified, and, with his arm around his wife's waist, said:

"It would be better if you left this house at once."

"I'm going," said Twm. "A pity I came here in the first place. I've seen things I never wanted to see."

He grabbed his bag and went off to school with the sound of Sioned's crying still in his ears. On the way he called on his friend, Arthur. He was having his breakfast of bacon and eggs.

"Hullo," he said, seeing Twm so pale and so early. "What's the matter?"

"Nothing," said Twm, "except that I got up very early and thought I'd like a stroll round the quay before going to school."

Arthur was shrewd enough not to accept this explanation, and soon Twm told him the whole story.

"Come home now and have some breakfast," said Arthur.

"No thanks, I don't feel like eating anything. But I'll have some dinner with you if you don't mind."

"You're welcome," said Arthur, who was a shopkeeper's son and knew there would be something for dinner every day.

"Remember, nobody is to know anything about this except you and Elin. I'll have to think up some story or other, but I'll go to Elin's for tea and tell her."

"Mam," said Arthur at dinner time, "can Twm have some dinner? His sister is quite poorly in bed."

"You're welcome my boy; what's the matter with your sister?"

"I don't know, but she's not very well."

"Well now, wouldn't it be better for you to stay here with Arthur until she's better?"

"We'll see," said Twm. "I'll go up there after school to see how she is."

"Yes, indeed, you have no time to waste looking after

yourself and this year such an important one for you at school."

Instead of going to tea at Sioned's, Twm went to Elin and told her everything.

"Well," said Elin, shaking her head, "I always said no good would come of that marriage. But we must keep this from mother."

"Of one thing I'm certain: I'll never go there to lodge again, even if Sioned and that little Corgi dog of hers begged me on their knees."

"Why?"

"I can't stand that Bertie. And their marriage is a fake. I wanted to thump him this morning, putting his hand around Sioned so tenderly and perhaps she's not the only one he's fondling."

"Twm!"

"Oh, perhaps I'm too suspicious. Better I didn't say any more. What shall we do? That's the question."

"Now, go to Arthur's until Saturday, seeing they're so hospitable, and then go to your old landlady to see if you can't go back there. Tell mother that you can't study at Sioned's because Eric is making too much noise."

Jane Gruffydd accepted Twm's excuse for changing his lodgings. It did not dawn on her that there was anything amiss in her daughter's house. When on the Saturday she asked how Sioned was, Twm had his answer ready. He said he had seen her the night before: but really he only saw her occasionally. When he went there to pay for his lodgings the Monday after his quarrel, Sioned was as haughty as Bertie, and she did not ask him to call again.

CHAPTER EIGHTEEN

Christmas was approaching – a festival that changes its meaning for parents as the children grow up. When the children were small, Christmas was a busy and happy time at Ffridd Felen. Everybody was preparing for the two-day Literary Festival. The children were happy because they would win prizes at the Festival, and they expected no other presents. Ann and Bob Ifans, Twnt i'r Mynydd, would come there on Christmas Eve and all the children would go to the festival together. Ann Ifans would bring some of her home-made toffee (*cyflath* was the word they used), and they would give her some of theirs to take home. The younger children always loved the night when the toffee was made. After they had gone to bed, their mother would come and place a lump of toffee in their mouths, warning them not to take it out in case it stained the bedclothes. If it was a big lump, that was very difficult; they had trouble turning it in their mouths, and their jawbones would ache the following morning.

But by 1908 things had changed. The older children had gone away, and Twm and Bet were too old for Christmas to give them much pleasure. Owen would be coming home, and Elin might come up on Christmas afternoon. Perhaps Sioned and her husband and the baby would come, but Jane did not look forward to that.

A few days before Christmas, she went into the town and on the way there she called on Elin.

"I don't know what to do about asking Sioned and her husband up for Christmas," she said.

"I don't think she'll come, you know," said Elin, who remembered the reason for Twm's departure.

"Don't you think so?"

"I'm sure. I heard her talking about staying at home and having a tea-party or something like that."

"Oh! And how are things with her, tell me."

"All right, as far as I know."

Jane Gruffydd's welcome in Sioned's house this time was not as warm as it used to be. Sioned was busy making pies.

"I'll make a cup of tea as soon as I've put these in the oven," she in a tone of voice that indicated she would rather not.

"There's no need for you to trouble yourself at all," said her mother. "I've promised to go round to Elin's."

Sioned cheered up at this.

"Wait a bit and I'll come and sit down with you."

While Sioned was in the scullery busy with her pies, her mother looked round the kitchen. It was not up to what it used to be. Everything looked shabby and dull, and Eric looked neglected, playing with a dirty old wooden horse. You could not say that the room was untidy, but there was no shine on anything.

Soon Sioned came into the room, wearing a black apron that was torn right across.

"I'm making some mince-pies," she said. "I've already made the cake."

"Cake? Are you making a cake as well as currant bread for Christmas?" asked her mother, crossly.

"No, it was currant bread I meant."

"Well, say what you mean, then."

Sioned took no notice of the rebuke, but went straight on; "Bertie's bringing a goose home tonight – a present from a friend of his."

"Lucky for you."

"We're going to have a lot of friends here on Christmas Day and the day after."

"You won't be able to come up to us then?"

"No, we shan't. Did anybody say we would?"

"No, nobody," she replied curtly.

"I thought Nel might have told you, she seems to think we should do everything she does."

"Elin didn't say a word to me," said Jane, hotly.

"We would have liked to come, but these friends of Bertie's are coming; they're very nice people."

"So that's that," said her mother. "I must go now."

She looked at Eric, who was sitting under the sewing-machine.

"Come here, my little dear, " she said, "for you to have some toffee."

Eric ran for the toffee and snatched it out of his grand-mother's hand.

"Say 'thank you'," said his mother.

Eric was busy looking inside the paper bag.

"Now, Eric, say 'thank you' to your grandmother for the toffee."

"Eric. Say 'thank you'."

Some of the toffee was already in Eric's mouth.

"Let him be," said his grandmother.

Jane Gruffydd had in her basket a pound of butter to give to Sioned, but she took it home with her.

She was in a bit of a temper when she reached Elin's place.

"I don't really know why I go there."

"Go where?" asked Elin.

"To see Sioned."

"What's the matter with her today?"

"I don't know. She was upitty about something. She didn't want to see me, for sure."

"Didn't she offer you some tea?"

"Yes, she asked me with an ill grace. But I told her I was coming to you."

"You did right."

"The devil take her, she and her mince pies and her cake and her goose."

"Is she going to have a goose?"

Elin stood poised in the act of cutting a slice of bread.

"Yes, Bertie is having one as a present, she said."

"Yes, I bet."

"And she says some of his friends are going there to tea on Christmas Day. Some very nice people."

"Yes, they are all very nice in Sioned's eyes if they speak English and wear bracelets."

"Tell me, are they able to pay their way?"

"Yes, so far as I know. He had a rise recently."

"It was just that I thought there was a shabby look about everything, and the little boy appeared uncared for."

"Yes, he does. She takes no pleasure in looking after him."

There was a hurt look in Jane Gruffydd's eyes as she went to catch the brake.

"I'll be up on Christmas Day."

"Yes, come as soon as you can."

The mother pulled her bit of fur closer round her neck. She wore the same coat as she had worn six years ago on the day of the prize-giving, and the same hat, but worn at a different angle.

CHAPTER NINETEEN

After dinner on Christmas Day, Owen and Twm were sitting in the best kitchen at Ffridd Felen putting the world to rights instead of going to the Literary Festival, as they had done when they were children. Inside, everything was comfortable, a cheerful fire in the grate and the furniture from Y Fawnog gleaming. Owen had managed to persuade his father to buy the furniture, after old Sioned Gruffydd died, and share the money between the children. Outside, everything looked grey and bleak. They had just finished an excellent dinner of roast potatoes and a pudding with a sweet sauce. In the morning the postman had called with a letter containing a postal order for ten shillings from Wiliam and a Christmas card in English from Sioned. Elin had come up in the afternoon.

A whole term had gone by since Owen and Twm had had opportunity to talk to each other, and Owen was very keen to pump Twm for information about Sioned, because he had seen the pained expression on his mother's face as she threw Sioned's card on the dresser. So it was this afternoon that he heard about the quarrel between Sioned and Twm, something that Twm had not put in a letter.

"Those two will come to a sticky end some day," said Owen.

"I don't care what happens to them," said Twm. "Everybody is worrying far too much about them. They have chosen the way they want to live, and everybody has forgotten how selfish she was with that money".

"Yes," said Owen, pondering what a strange thing a family was. Portraits of some of them looked down on him now from the wall. Sometimes he wished to smash them in order to forget his lineage. And yet it was impossible to cut himself off from them, as impossible as it was to cut himself off from the pain caused by some of those who were still alive. There they were, quarrelling and making up, then quarrelling again; he hated them enough sometimes to want to kill them. Many times during his college days Owen felt that he could have killed Sioned for playing such a dirty trick, and he scraping along on the bare necessities of life. But then when he saw Sioned he spoke to her without showing any sign of animosity. Why was it impossible to leave members of the family alone?

"It's no good worrying about it," said Twm as he saw him gazing into the fire.

"I wouldn't worry if I knew mother wasn't worrying. Does she know why you went from there?"

"No, but I have a feeling she thinks all is not well there. She was down there this week and didn't have much of a welcome."

"Shame..."

"Sioned was quite the lady, talking about her mince pies and goose."

"Can they afford things like that?"

"No, certainly not. They can't unless Bertie has had some luck on the horses."

Owen laughed.

"All the money must have gone by this time," he said.

"Very likely, and she'll be up here like a shot when there's nothing left."

"No, she won't," said Owen, "I'll see to that."

"Yes, but you won't be the one to decide, my lad. What should have been done at the time of the fuss over grandmother's will – and after finding out what Sioned intended doing with the money – was to tell her to keep her distance, and cut her off from the family."

"Perhaps so."

"But why must we meet trouble half way? We worry too

much about the family, instead of leaving them alone. I've stopped worrying about Sioned a long time ago."

"Yes, but it's difficult somehow."

"Some can. Sioned doesn't care how much pain she causes others, and why should we have to do our duty when she can't?"

"It would be a sad look-out for mother and father if we were all like Sioned."

"But the rest of us can do too much because one is doing too little."

Owen felt that there was a great deal of truth in Twm's words.

After tea, the two went for a walk along the lane. The countryside was a perfect picture of the greyness of winter; bare trees, russet fields, a grey sea, grey mist, and everything sodden underfoot.

"Do you like being home at this time of the year?" asked Twm.

"I like being in the house," said Owen, "but as for the district, here's a perfect picture of hopelessness. Who on earth thought of building a house in a place like this?"

"Someone who was trying to escape complete poverty, very likely: and we are still fleeing from poverty."

"I never thought of it that way," said Owen.

"How do you think we came here in the first place, then?"

"I suppose I must have thought we had always been here."

"Ask Aunt Geini to tell you the story of her grandmother, or father's grandmother as far as that goes, our great grandmother. We came from over there," said Twm pointing his finger towards Lleyn, "from the same place as mother came afterwards."

Later on, Twm said, "I've entered an *englyn* for the meet tonight."

Owen looked at him with admiration. He was a tall, handsome lad.

They went to the Literary Meeting that night; it was particulary interesting for them both. The chapel was full and the air was warm; the lamps gleamed and there was a cheerful look on everybody's face. Everything seemed the same as it has been ten years before – the same piece of calico along the front of the stage with "Moel Arian and District Literary and Music Festival" on it in bold blue and red letters, the same smell of varnish from the seats and children shuffling their feet; the smell of oranges and the officials on the stage wearing the same old ribbons.

Twm won the prize for his poem, and from then on until the end the two enjoyed everything in the meeting – the singing and recitation (really they were of very indifferent quality), the impromptu speech (that was comical), judging the baskets, the stockings and oatcakes (that was interesting), and the choirs putting a joyful seal on the whole festival.

The end of the holidays drew near. To Owen, the best thing about them was that he was at home, had nothing to do, and could spend his time quietly chatting. Since September he had been Latin master in Tre Ffrwd: after three years at College, he had graduated with second class honours in Latin.

The College had not left much of a mark on him. Perhaps the blame for this was as much his as the College's. He had made friends, had talked and argued with his room-mates, had worried over his work, and worked out how to live on next to nothing. He'd taken no part in games, for that cost money, and he'd averted his eyes from the smart young girls who thronged the College halls. But now he regretted not having shared in so many of the College activities. His degree would not have been any the worse for it. But at that time the lack of money forced him to keep his nose to the grindstone. Now that he had a post he intended to keep it, and the only way to do that was to work hard.

So he had still to sacrifice many pleasures; and he saved money. He always remembered his father's low wages, and the mounting bills in the shops, and from his monthly salary of ten pounds, he managed to send three pounds home. The other bachelor masters in the school enjoyed themselves. They went to Liverpool on Saturdays and paid to see plays and go to concerts. The married ones were forced to economise. They wore old clothes in school and kept a best suit until Sunday. They strove to educate their children and tried to buy some books. The work at school became a matter of routine to them. They made little effort, gave no fresh lessons, and they had their own method of marking exercises without reading them through. They laughed at a youngster like Owen, who prepared his lessons and carried books home to mark.

"You'll get fed up with that," they said.

"Perhaps," said Owen. "Probably you were like me when you were my age."

He did not want his headmaster to find fault with him in his first term at least.

At this time he did not have much opportunity of doing anything else but work; and he couldn't afford to enjoy himself like the other single masters.

As the time drew near for him to return after the Christmas holiday, Owen wondered whether it would always be like this. A rise in salary for a teacher was a matter of luck or chance in those days. His mother would clear her debts in the shops some day. But perhaps Twm would not win a scholarship to college. He had the ability, but he seemed so unconcerned about his work, and about his family. He wondered whether Twm would put his shoulder under the burden after finishing college and getting a post. He doubted it, and yet there was a good deal of truth in what Twm had said about family ties on Christmas Day, that it was possible for some to do too much. But there it was, that was how a man was born, most likely, one with a conscience and one without. And then it dawned on him that these things would not come to trouble him if everybody did his duty. It was Sioned's failure that made him complain about doing his share. When everybody pulled his weight, no one could find fault with another. There was much to be said for Twm's suggestion that Sioned should be cut off from the family.

And so Owen mulled over things like this in his mind before setting off to take up his work again. His mother was happier than she had been on Christmas Day. Gradually, she would be able to pay off more of the bills in the shops.

CHAPTER TWENTY

On a Monday morning in June, 1912, Jane Gruffydd was washing clothes, thinking about this and that but more especially about the letters from the boys. Twm had gone to college in 1910 on a slightly better scholarship than Owen's, but because he could not enter the education department without first having been a pupil teacher, he was worse off.

Bet had gone into service so that Ifan and Jane were by this time completely on their own. Thirty-two years had gone by since their marriage and they were growing old. There was always a tired look about Ifan and he was not able to do much work on the small-holding in the evening. It took Jane much longer to get through her household duties, and she frequently rested. She would have liked to have kept Bet at home. Their hair was turning grey, their bodies becoming ungainly, and their eyes somewhat dimmed. In the emptiness of their lives there was emotional disturbance which did not happen when the children were home. Life had gone on placidly, with none of this thinking of what the postman would bring. Letters came from the boys every week. Not one of them would have any news to tell, but even saying that filled up some part of the paper. Twm's letters were fullest; there seemed to be more happening in a college than in a coalpit or school. Frequently his letters would describe the financial strains of the college and he usually finished with a diffident appeal to his mother to slip him something on the side.

Wiliam returned home from the south every summer. He looked well in a dark blue suit, which was a sure sign to the people of Moel Arian that he was living a respectable life and he had not 'gone to the dogs'. He spoke of the South as if it was next to Heaven. There were good wages to be had there. Most of the colliers believed in the Union and the Labour Party was growing in strength. He wore a white satin muffler, and this emphasised the pallor of his cheeks. And yet, as the end of his fortnight's holiday drew near, he would speak less about the South and would go and lie in the fields and gaze in the direction of the sea.

It was of Twm that the mother was thinking most this morning because she was washing his clothes, and because he was in the middle of his examinations. She wondered how he was getting on in such sultry weather as this.

It was eleven o'clock and the day was heavy and sunless. She was regretting deeply that she had not been able to keep Bet at home – if only to have somebody to make her a cup of tea now and then. She was hungry but felt too hot and listless to go and prepare a meal. She heard the click of the farmyard gate, and she was not worried by it; she would welcome a chat with anybody. The footsteps approached the cowshed, where the washing was done in summer, and to her amazement who was there but Elin, and one look at her was enough to know that she was the bearer of bad news.

"What's the matter?" said the mother.

"Don't excite yourself; come into the house," said Elin.

In the darkness of the kitchen, it was impossible to see anything.

Elin poked the fire into life.

"Sioned is in trouble."

"What is it?"

"Bertie has run away."

"Has what?"

Jane Gruffydd slowly lowered herself into a chair and Elin shook the kettle to see if there was any water in it. Then she placed it on the fire and sat down.

"Yes, he has run away."

Jane Gruffydd was dumbfounded; she could think of

nothing to say. But presently she said, "It's only a week since they were up here," she said, as if Bertie had died and not run away.

"He was at work as usual Saturday morning," said Elin, "and then went to the station. From there he sent a boy with a message for Sioned, to say that he had been called away suddenly on business, and that he would be home on Sunday evening without fail. But he didn't come. Saturday afternoon, his employer checked the accounts and there was thirty pounds missing. He came up to tell Sioned this morning."

"Did you see Sioned?"

"No. A woman who lives near her came to tell me, and I thought it better to come here to you than go to Sioned, in case you heard about it from someone else, because the news will spread here like wildfire."

"Oh, yes," said the mother, who shut her eyes, and sighed.

"What a disgrace for us, and the boys, and after they've had a good education too. I won't be able to raise my head in this place again."

"It's a disgrace for nobody but himself. Every sane person knows you couldn't help it."

"Perhaps, but a lot of people will be glad that we've been taken down a peg."

"Don't worry about them. We know what kind of people they are."

Elin began to prepare tea. Rattling the tea-cups gave a relief to feelings that had been seething inside her.

"The rotten little rascal," she said. "But come and have a cup of tea, and eat as if nothing's happened."

Jane tried to do that. The thought came to her how wonderful it would be to drink this cup of tea with Elin and not have anything trouble her.

"The biggest worry," said Elin, "is what to do about Sioned and the boy; I'm sure they haven't a penny."

This was the first time for Jane Gruffydd to look at it from this point of view. She had only thought of the disgrace, the gossip, and satisfaction it would give to some.

But there was one more thing to cause her distress.

Once she had begun to view things correctly, the mother became practical.

"Well now," she said, "Twm must not hear a word of this until his exams are over."

"No," said Elin, "but it will be surprising if he doesn't hear about it, for there are many lads from town there in the College. But I can go to Arthur and warn him not to say anything."

"Yes, that would be best."

"Because Twm is so much against Sioned," said Elin.

And then she took the opportunity to give an account of Twm's departure from Sioned's house.

"Heavens above!" said Jane Gruffydd. "There's no knowing how much lack of food she's suffered because of that rascal."

"A bit of that won't do her any harm," said Elin. "She jibbed at some good food at home. The little boy is the one to be pitied; he'll have a rough upbringing, I'm afraid."

"Well," said Jane Gruffydd, "it's no use talking about it. I suppose the best thing for me to do is to go down to see her."

"Wait until tomorrow and then you can have a ride down. I'll go there today and you stay at home and discuss with Dad what's the best thing to do."

"No," said Jane Gruffydd, "I'll come down with you. I can't stay here all afternoon, and it's no use sending for your father in the quarry, and you mustn't impose too much on your mistress's generosity."

She set about preparing to go.

"Now then," she said, "because Twnt i'r Mynydd is too far, I'll go and tell Jane Williams what's happened so that she can tell Ifan if he happens to come home from the quarry before I get back. Everybody is sure to come to know about it sooner or later, and I'd rather tell her myself. She'll have fewer lies with the news that way."

When her mother was closing the gate to Jane Williams' house Elin noticed how care-worn she looked, and as she turned away from the gate there was a strange look in her eyes.

Jane Gruffydd went on her own to see Sioned. After walking down in the heat of the day, her legs were trembling as she approached her daughter's house. She thought of all her visits to the town; not one of them seemed to be free of some trouble or other. But this was a different kind of trouble, much worse than the bother over the price of pigs or things like that.

Sioned, Eric, and some woman were having tea. Sioned's manner changed when she saw her mother.

"Oh, you have company," said Jane Gruffydd.

"This is Bertie's mother," said Sioned.

Jane Gruffydd did not really know what to make of Bertie's mother. She wore ear-rings and had three or four rings on her fingers – rather grubby fingers whatever her ears were like. She did not appear to be worrying much about her son. She continued to eat unconcernedly clicking her tongue now and again on one of her front teeth. She had some well-worn slippers on her feet, which slapped the floor as she ate. Afterwards she sat back in the armchair and Jane Gruffydd noticed that there was not much distance between her armpits and her waist, if she had any waist at all.

Sioned handed her mother a cup, and poured some tea.

"This is a fine pickle, indeed," Jane Gruffydd said to herself, "I'd better not say anything."

"Did you walk down, Mrs Gruffydd?" asked Mrs Elis, Bertie's mother.

"Yes, indeed, through the heat, and I had to leave the washing and everything else."

"Really, there was no need for you to rush down like that," said Sioned.

"No, indeed. You see, I'm here to look after her," said Mrs Elis.

"I thought she might like to see her mother."

"Oh, Janet will have every fair play," said Bertie's mother.

"From whom?" said Jane Gruffydd suddenly. "It's obvious she won't have any fair play from her husband."

"Oh, yes she will. Bertie will come back, you'll see," said his mother.

"If he's coming back, why did he have to go in the first place?" asked Jane Gruffydd.

"You see, Mrs Gruffydd," said Bertie's mother, "people are telling lies; nobody can tell the truth nowadays. I believe Bertie has gone on business as he said in his note."

"I certainly hope so, but what about the money in Davies and Johnson's?"

"Oh, don't mention Davies and Johnson to me," said Bertie's mother, "they are very suspicious people. Perhaps it's all a mistake."

"I truly hope so," said Jane.

"Oh, I'm sure of it, Mrs Gruffydd," said Bertie's mother, rubbing her hands with their rings on the arms of the chair, and crossing her legs. "Nobody knows Bert better than his mother," and she clicked her tongue on the tooth again.

Instinctively, Jane Gruffydd looked at her own left hand, her wedding-ring shining from having been immersed in soap-suds, and the skin of her hand glistening, with blue veins standing out.

She turned her ring with her thumb as she always did when in a quandary. She had not decided yet what to do about asking Sioned to come home with her. She would have liked to have discussed it with Ifan. But seeing Bert's mother there, filling the armchair and putting on airs, she did not want her at any rate, to think more of her son than she did of her daughter, and she wanted to show her that Sioned had as good a home and parents as Bert.

"Would you like to come home for a bit with Eric?" asked Jane Gruffydd.

"Oh, you needn't bother, Mrs Gruffydd; I'll do my best for Janet," said Mrs Elis, butting in.

Sioned took no notice of her mother-in-law, and turning towards her mother, said, "No, I won't come up just yet, anyway. I'll have to be here when Bertie returns."

"Well, that's sensible enough," said her mother, "but we'll see. But since Mrs Elis is here with you, I'd like to be home before your father comes from the quarry."

"Will you have transport?" asked Mrs Elis.

"Not on a Monday like this."

"Look, Grandma," said Eric who was now by the sewing-machine. "Look what I've got!"

"Bring it here for Grandma to see," said Jane Gruffydd.

He ran with his little train to show it to her.

"I want Daddy to send me a tricycle from away."

"Do you really? Well, here's something for you," said his country grandmother, giving him sixpence.

"Thank you," said Eric, not having to be prompted this time.

Jane Gruffydd was more fortunate than usual on her way back. She had a lift for a good part of the way in the carriage belonging to the vet who was going in that direction.

She lit a fire and fried some bacon and eggs before Ifan arrived home, and she let her husband finish eating before breaking the news to him. As usual, Ifan withdrew into himself, too overcome to say anything. He did not move from the house all evening. He had planned to cut some June hay for the cattle but he let them manage the best they could on the poor pasture until the next day. He, for his part, was considering what the people in the quarry would say, and it hurt him to think of all his hard-earned money being squandered, and by strangers at that. Seeing her husband so quiet, Jane thought it would not do for her to be the same.

"Look here," she said, "I've decided that I'm not going to worry this."

"How is it possible not to?" said he.

"By remembering that something worse could have happened," said she. "Sioned could have died."

"For all I know that might have been better."

"No, indeed not. There would have been countless things to worry about then. That we hadn't bothered to find out about her earlier, and thinks like that."

"Sioned has never brought us anything but pain."

"True, but this time it's not her fault."

"It was her fault to marry that worm of a fellow."

"Perhaps so, but few people know each other before marriage. Many men would like to leave their wives if they could."

"But Bertie wasn't running away from Sioned."

"Well, the fact is that he has run away, whatever the reason."

For a long time they sat by the fire without lighting the lamp. After a dark, sultry day, the sun came out in the late evening and went down into the Irish Sea like a ball of fire, raising its head once more before sinking beneath the waves.

"We'd better go to bed and wait to see what tomorrow will bring," said Jane.

And at that there came a gentle tap on the door and Geini entered, having difficulty in seeing the two sitting like shadows under the great chimney.

"More trouble, Geini," said Jane.

"Well, yes," she said. "Is it true that he's run off with some girl?"

"Is that what people are saying?"

"That's what I've heard people saying around here."

"No, he hasn't," said Ifan. "Nobody knows more than that

136

he's run away, and there's a mistake in the accounts."

"Have you been to town then?" his sister asked Ifan.

"No. I went," said Jane, and proceeded to give an account of her journey and a description of Bertie's mother.

"They sound like a right lot of 'don't care a damns' to me, I must say," said Geini.

"Yes, I thought myself far superior to her."

Geini and Ifan laughed at this.

They felt better after Geini had been.

Bertie never did come back. It was taken for granted that he had gone to America.

What worried them most of all was what was going to happen to Sioned and Eric. That was the only thing that troubled Twm and Owen. Wiliam was too far away and his holidays too short for all this to have much effect on him. The other two boys saw all their holidays being spoiled if Sioned and her child came to live at Ffridd Felen. And who was to pay for her keep? But neither of them dared say anything in a letter. They knew only too well their mother's generosity of hand and heart, and they knew too how much she disliked others interfering in something that concerned her personally.

It was Elin who settled the problem in the end. Every night she had off, she went to see Sioned and saw her becoming more and more poverty-stricken, without plan at all but listlessly talking about expecting Bertie home.

"Well, you can wait years for him," she said, "but it's obvious his family don't want to do anything for you, and it would be too much to expect Mother and Father to do anything to help you."

"I wouldn't go back to live in the country for a pension," said Sioned.

"Well, since you think so much of the townspeople," said said Elin, "you'd better ask for their help."

"How?"

"Well, I'd sell this furniture, and take a small room somewhere and sew. I'll mention it to my mistress and ask her if she can bring work for you."

"What shall I do with Eric?"

"Perhaps he can go home for a while, until you earn enough to set up house for yourself again."

And that plan was agreed upon.

By the time Owen and Wiliam came home for their holidays, Eric was already there, looking healthier and better dressed and enjoying himself with the other children of the district. Twm was home for a month before the other boys and had become fairly used to his nephew. But at first he was annoyed with his mother for having taken Eric, and he showed his disapproval by being very prickly with his nephew. He could not bear the noise he made running with his toys on the slat pavement.

"Go somewhere else to play," he said to the child, crossly. This was about the sixth time for his mother to hear him say this.

"Look here," she said, "nobody is going to be nasty to that little child while he's here. If he is to be here, he can stay without anybody reproaching him."

Twm went out to cry. He had been working hard for his examinations after neglecting his work all the year by reading things that had nothing to do with his course.

CHAPTER TWENTY-ONE

When Wiliam came home in 1913, he brought with him a wife, that same dark-eyed girl who had been so amused by his embarrassment over washing himself in the tub when he first went to the South.

The same year, Twm graduated with second-class honours in Welsh. He failed to get a post in a Secondary School, and rather than be without a post at all, he went to teach in a Primary School in Llan Ddol, not far from his home. For over six months he had to exist on a salary lower than that of a qualified teacher, because he had had no experience of teaching before going to college.

He was fairly happy during the holidays. The fact that he had a post at all raised his spirits somewhat. Owen told him that he was bound to get a place in a Secondary School after having some experience at a Primary School, so long as he did not stay too long at Llan Ddol.

These were the happiest holidays for Jane and Ifan Gruffydd since Owen went to college. From now on they would not have to pay anything out for the boys, and they would be able to speed up the repayment of their debts to the shops.

Nobody in Ffridd Felen knew anything of Wiliam's marriage until about a fortnight before he came home. And that was a good thing, for Jane had that much less time to wonder what kind of person her daughter-in-law would be.

From the moment they saw her they all liked Poli. Her eyes were darker than bilberries with a tinge of blue in the whites. Her hair was black as a raven's feathers and just as straight. To her, Ffridd Felen and Moel Arian were like new toys to a child, and to someone brought up amidst houses and the noise of coalpits, there was some delightful new discovery lurking in every corner. She never stopped speaking, not caring whether anyone understood her strange dialect or not, and she laughed gleefully, showing her red tongue, at anything she did not understand in the Gruffydd's speech. She got up early, helped her mother-in-law, and showed clearly that she did not want Wiliam's holiday to cause more work for anybody. Indeed, there was less work for everybody because of Poli; she saw the task to be done and did it without being asked.

Sioned came up over the Bank Holiday, and Poli worked harder but spoke less; she regarded Sioned with awe. By this time, Sioned was beginning to find her feet in the sewing business, and this showed rather in her own clothes than in offering to help towards Eric's keep. Tight skirts were coming into fashion and Sioned could hardly walk in hers. With the high white collar to her blouse, and the little black hat turned down over her face like a toadstool, she looked very regal. To Poli she was like a queen, but she breathed more freely when Sioned had gone.

One Saturday, Ifan and Jane Gruffydd, Wiliam, Poli and Eric went to Lleyn to visit the Sarn Goch family. Poli was the instigator of the expedition. One thing she could not understand about her mother-in-law and the people of Moel Arian generally, was that they were such stick-in the-muds. She frequently told her mother-in-law that she kept too much to the house.

"But where should I go?" asked Jane Gruffydd.

"Anywhere. It doesn't matter where."

And so Wiliam and she planned a visit to Sarn Goch one Saturday and paid everybody's expenses.

Jane Gruffydd frequently looked back on that Saturday. That was the last time for her to see her parents alive, for they had been buried by the end of the year. But Jane had an opportunity to tell her mother that things were beginning to improve for her, and that they would soon be able to repay some of the money they had borrowed from her parents from time to time.

"There's no need for you," she said. "I shan't live long, and you might as well not repay the debt as for us to leave the money to you when we're gone."

And that's exactly how the will was.

When the summer holidays of 1914 came, Poli could no longer suggest a visit to Lleyn, and the Great War prevented any other expeditions.

When the war broke out, nobody in Moel Arian knew what to make of it. They did not understand its causes; they believed in what the papers said, that Great Britain was going to the help of smaller nations. But they began to feel the effects right from the first day, for the smaller quarries in the area shut down. In fact, one closed before the war started. It was generally believed that the war could not last long. Nobody in Moel Arian, or Ffridd Felen, thought that the war could affect them personally; war was something for soldiers and politicians. They expected everything to go up in price and quoted the story of the old woman who had raised the price of mint during the Franco-Prussian war. The Ffridd Felen children remembered the South African war, and how the headmaster had made them march up through the village in procession with their banners flying when Mafeking was relieved, but it had not meant anything to them. A man here and there belonged to the Militia, but that was not something to be proud of. The Militiaman was rather an object of scorn, and the same was true when the first army uniform was seen in Moel Arian in 1914, although its colour was different from that of the militia.

Neither Owen nor Twm thought that the war would have any effect on them. Wiliam and Poli returned to the South without having been able to get about much. But that was only because of some vague uneasiness.

Twm still continued to teach in the Llan Ddol Elementary School, having utterly failed to get a post in a Secondary School. He was on the short list for one post and the headmaster had told him, while regretting that he could not offer him the post, that it would be better for him to give up his present post in the Elementary School, because it could only be a hindrance to his getting a post in a Secondary School. But that was impossible now with his father out of work once again.

So it was back to the same old place once more with the prospect of a pound a month increase in salary. But that was small recompense measured against his dislike of his work. He was not over-fond of teaching children at the best of times, but having to teach them under the conditions that prevailed in Llan Ddol school was absolute hell to him. He had to teach a class of sixty in the same room as another class of sixty. The entrance to the infants school was beneath the window of his classroom, and four times a day the little ones would troop out before the end of his lessons. The worst thing of all, though, was the headmaster's desk being in the same room, so he was constantly under the eye of that hawk. The headmaster beat the pupils mercilessly. They were sent there from other classes, so that Twm's pupils spent the day gazing at punishments being handed out. Every morning, with a long pliable cane, the headmaster would punish the latecomers, and this with the words of his prayers hardly out of his mouth. Twm's blood boiled at the injustice of it all. The hawk would descend suddenly on his class for no other reason than that he was in a bad temper. To cap it all, Twm was allowed no opportunity of using his knowledge of Welsh, and he was forced to teach subjects he knew little about.

As 1914 went on, more and more of the khaki suits were to be seen. There was an air of seriousness abroad and things were changing from day to day. Twm felt very restless. He wanted to get about, but, after sending a little bit home, he had very little money left, and there was nothing to do in Llan Ddol. Sometimes he spent a week-end in Bangor with Ceinwen, who was in her third year at the College, and he was able to see some of his contemporaries among the students. On every visit he would hear about one of his contemporaries having joined the forces, and the students themselves were flocking to the colours.

On a Friday in January, 1915, the school was more hateful than usual. It had been raining hard all day and Twm's classroom was full of the smell of wet clothes drying. Although the children had not been able to go out during the afternoon break, they were not allowed to go home any earlier. Twm decided to go to Bangor although he had been there the previous week-end. The attraction of joining-up was growing all the time. When he arrived in Bangor that night, he learned that Arthur, his old school friend, had given up his research to join the forces. On the Saturday morning the entrance halls of the college were half empty, and there was no conversation to be had with anybody except women students, and they were full of fuss and excitement because somebody or other had joined up, while some, a few of them, were sad. That night, Twm with two of his friends who were still at the college, Bob Huws and Dai Morgan, went to 'The Black Lion' and there, over their beers, the three decided to join the army. To put a seal on their decision, they drank some more beer and Twm composed a scurrilous englyn on the subject of his headmaster. They then staggered back to their lodgings and Twm slept on the sofa in the parlour. The following morning they regretted their decision, but to Twm it became more and more attractive as Monday morning drew near.

On the Monday morning the headmaster came to him to point out some mistake in his register for the previous Friday. The smells of that afternoon came back to Twm, and he remembered the circumstances under which the register had been filled. The blood came rushing to his head.

He threw his chalk on to the desk, put on his coat, and walked out of the school without having given a single lesson. He did not dare look back for he knew that if he saw the disappointed look on the faces of the girls in the front row, he would be tempted to return.

There was a spirit of adventure abroad, and his world was too confined. He had always felt himself walled-in, but this morning the walls were falling down. He would be able to see something of the great outside, something other than these eternal mountains, and the sour face of his headmaster.

CHAPTER TWENTY-TWO

Thursday morning, as Eric was putting on his cap before going to school, the postman was heard at the gate, and he ran to meet him.

"There's a letter, Grandma. Ta-ta, I'm going now."

"Ta-ta. I wonder who's written today. It's Twm's handwriting. But the postmark...? Have you seen my glasses, Ifan?"

"Here they are."

Jane sat in the chair, her face white.

"What's the matter?" asked Ifan.

"Read that."

His lips trembled too. He walked out, leaned against the doorpost and stared towards Anglesey.

When he returned, his wife was crying.

"Oh," she said, "but children are cruel."

"Yes," he said, gazing into the fire. "I think it would be better if I went to look for work somewhere."

"No," she said, "you'd better not, not for the time being anyway."

"I can't see how we're going to manage now."

"We've seen worse times than this."

"I don't know; things are costing more now."

"Other things will go up in price as a result," she said. "Pigs and things like that, and we've only Eric to keep now."

"And Sioned should give us something towards that from now on."

"Yes, she should, but we ought to know Sioned by this time."

The next week, Twm's clothes and books arrived from Llan Ddol. His mother folded his clothes carefully and put

145

them in a drawer in his bedroom. She took some of the china from the bottom shelf of the dresser in the living-room and put his books there. She glanced through some of them but did not understand them.

At the end of the month she received five pounds from Twm – his pay for the period he'd worked. She put the money in a box to await his return home.

When Owen heard of Twm's decision, his anger welled up, but he did not write to him while he was in that frame of mind. His own salary had not increased, whilst prices rose. His landlady had already hinted that she would expect eleven shillings a week for his two rooms. And here was Twm playing such a shabby trick! When he could be sending a little money home each month, he had gone and joined the army where he would not be getting enough to pay for the little comforts he desired. It was true that he had had an unpleasant headmaster. He deserved a far better post. But after all he should remember his father and mother. Then he remembered the discussion they had had the first Christmas after he had obtained a post in Tre Ffrwd, and Twm saying that it was possible to worry too much about the family. So far Twm had not shown that he was worrying at all. At any rate, he had not enlisted because he was fed up with helping his family. No, Owen remembered his restlessness in the town; his desire to explore and get to know things without the help of books. The world was too narrow for him. He had never been able to sit down in the house after composing a piece of poetry.

"Come for a walk to the top of the mountain," he had said once at Ffridd Felen after writing some poetry, "so that we can find some space to shake our legs. Owen remembered that now... the scream of the lapwing; the moon reflected in dark peat water; the lamps of the town like a cluster of gems on the river's edge; the lights of Holyhead winking in the distance, and the top of Snowdon majestic and clear in the moonlight.

Before Owen wrote, he received a letter from Twm from somewhere on the English border. He did not sound happy, and as far as Owen could gather this was because Bob Huws and Dai Morgan had not kept their word and had refused to go with Twm to enlist. He had almost gone back to the school, but he knew that the door there would be closed to him. The people around him now were all strangers.

Owen did not have the heart to rebuke him in his letter. Everybody thought the war would not last very long and there would be no need for anybody who joined now to leave the country.

The summer holidays of 1915 were very troubled ones for Jane Gruffydd. Wiliam and Poli were at Ffridd Felen and this time brought with them a little girl, six months old. Owen was at home and so was Bet for a while. Owen was completely lost without Twm and he had no money to go anywhere. Bet kept saying she would like to go away to work in an ammunition factory. Twm had mentioned some time before that he was expecting some leave shortly and that he might arrive home suddenly, but on the other hand, it might be postponed until September. His mother did not know what she would like best. She longed to see him, and yet she would prefer to have him to herself when there would be no 'fuss and bother' there, as she said.

One Saturday afternoon, she, Wiliam, Ifan, Eric, Poli and the baby went over to Anglesey. For the life of her Jane could not help but contrast this day with that visit to Lleyn two years before. They saw Moel Arian and the quarries from across the water, and she longed to be back there having a hot fresh cup of tea under her own roof. But she dared not suggest going back. Apart from Ifan and herself they all seemed to be enjoying themselves. Somehow, Ifan looked completely ill at ease. He was irritated by the fuss Wiliam and Poli made with the baby, and with having to watch Eric throwing stones into the water. The steamer which plied its trade across the straits left infrequently, as did the buses which had just begun to travel in the Moel Arian direction. When they finally got to the Square in town, they found a large number of people waiting for buses, and among them were many soldiers in khaki, some on their own, others talking and laughing with young women. They, themselves, waited for the bus to arrive.

In front of them stood a tall soldier with his back to them, and Poli said, "Look here, there's a smart soldier for you."

The soldier turned, and smiled.

"Well, Twm!" said everybody at once.

Walking home the mile after leaving the bus, Jane Gruffydd noticed the great difference between the way Twm and his father walked.

The days went by like the wind, and Twm slipped from his mother's grasp the same way. She could never get used to him in that old khaki, and could not be convinced that he was not allowed to wear civilian clothes. To her, this uniformed figure was not Twm. And yet it was Twm who talked, laughed and ate. But it was not possible to have him to herself as it used to be when he came over from Llan Ddol for the week-end. At meal-times there was a crowd at the dining-table and she could not encourage him to eat as she would have liked.

She had pickled some herrings, the small ones you could get in August. They ate them with new potatoes, oatmeal bread, and buttermilk.

"Oh," said Twm, sighing after he had eaten, "that was a good meal."

"Do you have good food in the Army?" asked his mother.

"That meal would have been a real feast there," he replied.

And so the days went by.

When he was about to leave, Twm said, "If you ever have ten minutes to mix a cake, remember me." And Jane felt that she could express her feelings by sending food to her son.

He came again for Christmas and he and Owen had endless conversations. By this time, many more from the neighbourhood had joined-up, and in the Literary Festival there were many soldiers, men from the district, home on leave. Nobody thought that any of these would go into action. It was while talking to Twm that the fear first came to Owen. Yes, Twm was fairly certain that he would be going abroad. He was fed up with this country and hoped to go to Egypt or any other eastern country. Because his parents had not mentioned it, Owen thought it best for them to remain in the dark. Indeed, Twm's training had lasted so long by this time that the parents thought it would be always like this.

In May, Twm returned home without a word of warning and said that he had come unexpectedly because he had exchanged his leave with another. He was his usual happy self but showed no inclination to visit people. He pottered around the house, or went with his father to work in the fields; and because there was nobody else home, his mother came with him. The potato shoots were beginning to emerge dark green from the soil, and the grass was springing up, already green and thick where the ground had been manured. They watched the hen with her newly-hatched chicks. How prettily they ran after their mother through the grass, little yellow lumps, and the three laughed heartily at them. Twm felt like stretching out his hands and gathering them all up. Some, comically, were trying to spread their half-formed wings.

But in chapel on Sunday, Twm felt quite dispirited. His mother was there (she rarely went to the Church now), his father, Eric and himself. The chapel doors were open and the plaintive bleats of lambs could be heard with an occasional cock crowing in the distance. It was a prayer meeting, and Twm knew what to expect as the meeting went on. He felt a shiver of fear when he heard one of them add, "And remember the boys fighting on land and sea." The singing was poor because so many of the men had gone away. Towards the end, one of the deacons referred to "Thomas Gruffydd," saying that they were glad to see him home and looking so well, and wherever he had to go, they hoped to see him again soon, and may God protect him. On the way out, Twm noticed that there wasn't a press of people in the porch, or a rush to get out as there used to be.

"And how are you then?"

"You are looking well!"

"I hope you don't have to go overseas."

Twm was anxious to get away and he hurried home by challenging Eric to a race. He looked forward to his supper for he knew there would be cold meat and warmed-up potatoes. One thing he had always liked about Sunday night was – it did not matter if they returned even at seven – that they would have supper as soon as they arrived.

Eric thought the world of being allowed to walk beside his Uncle Twm. He was fascinated to see him cleaning his buttons and put on his cap.

"Pity Owen isn't here too," thought Twm, eating his supper. It would be impossible to see him this time, but he was sure to see him again sometime.

On the fourth day he went back. He really had one day left, but he wanted to see Ceinwen on the way. Sometimes he thought of telling his mother about her, but he wasn't sure how she'd take it. There would be plenty of time later to tell her, and after all perhaps another would be his wife.

He appeared most unconcerned as he prepared to leave. He sang some camp songs, to Eric's great delight.

"When are you coming again, Uncle Twm?"

"Hay-making time."

"Is that a long time?"

"No, not very long. Ta-ta Eric."

"Ta-ta."

"I wouldn't mind coming to the station with you," said his mother. "Those buses are so handy nowadays."

"Yes, do come, he said."

"And look," she said, "I kept your last pay for you. It's all there. Take some of it with you."

He nearly broke down at this point.

"Well, all right, I'll take a pound," he said, "because one buys more things during the summer. But you spend the rest."

"No; they'll be there when you come back."

"Well, goodbye, Dad."

"Goodbye, Twm, and good luck."

"I'll see you again during the hay-making, I'm sure."

"Good, and I hope that this old war will be over by then."

Twm in a way regretted having allowed his mother to accompany him to the town. Saying goodbye was a long-drawn-out business, he would have preferred to say goodbye to her in her homely apron than to see her on the town station, and thinking of her lonely journey back to Moel Arian. But it was true that the buses were very convenient now.

On the station he wished he could take hold of her hand, but he didn't. He put his head out of the window and watched her walking along the platform. Reaching the far end, she turned and waved her hand. He waved and continued to watch until the bridge hid her from view. He noticed how old-fashioned were her skirt and coat as she stood on the far end of the platform.

Within a few days, Owen had a letter from Twm confirming his fears that he was going overseas.

...I had hoped to see you, but it was impossible. I only had five days leave, four of which I spent at home and the last with Ceinwen. I did not tell them at home that I had five days because I didn't wish to hurt them. I thought once of sending for you to come, but mother and father would have then guessed that I was on embarkation leave. They seemed to be very happy. I don't believe they suspected that I was going away, and Eric is a great comfort to them by this time. I went to see Elin, Bet and Sioned. I felt very soft and forgiving at the time. Somehow bits of the old life do not fit in to this new life. Sioned appears to be very prosperous. She gets plenty of work, altering ready-made clothes for the shops, and she's still pretty. She seemed pleased to see me.

It's absolute chaos in this camp; everybody is packing. I can hardly believe that I was immersed in the silence of Moel Arian only three days ago. Everywhere was lovely. I realised that it was years since I had been at home in May. I hated leaving, but very likely, if it had been peacetime, and I had to live there, I wouldn't think much of it. It was grand to have plenty of time to watch the hen and her chicks, and to feel the warmth rising from the ground. It was very peaceful and relaxed, with very few people around. Isn't it a pity that we do not have enough time to watch the hens, and sheep and dogs, and not worry about anything?"

I went to the top of the mountain one night, but it wasn't a patch on that night we went there after I had written some poetry. When I was there, I thought of things Bet and I did as children – catching sticklebacks, putting bilberries on blades of grass and eating them (even now I can feel the roughness of the grass setting my teeth on edge), and pulling rushes from their sheaths in the ground, seeing who would get the longest ones and then plaiting them around our heads.

I'm looking now at my bed in the hut. I've slept in it for months, and although it isn't as soft as the one at home I've become very fond of it for it was so good to tumble into after a day of walking and marching. Have you ever thought what a wonderful thing a bed is? But someone else will be sleeping in it tonight. I wonder who? Perhaps it'll be a nice person, perhaps a scoundrel. It makes no difference. He too will have to leave it and someone else take his place; I'll feel sad thinking about that tonight, wherever I'll be.

John Twnt i'r Mynydd has also joined up – fed up with his old employer. He has been working his employees into the ground, and resurrecting things that had been in the shop since before the flood and selling them at exorbitant prices.

Good luck to them and their scramble for money.

I don't know where we're going. I had hoped to the East, but now I would just as soon go to France. If I'm wounded, then I'll be able to come back to this country. Well, a boot has just sailed past my head. I hope to see you before long.

Farewell, until the day comes round,
When we shall both be homeward bound.

As usual,

Twm

CHAPTER TWENTY-THREE

It was a great shock to Jane and Ifan Gruffydd that Twm was in France. The possibility of someone like Twm having to go into action had never occurred to them. They had always thought the war would be over before that.

From that time, a dark cloud hung over their lives, and they felt as if they were just waiting for it to break. Somehow they thought it would never clear. Their greatest trial was waiting for the post and expecting a letter. After receiving one, they would be happy for a few days; then their hearts would begin to ache again.

The mother baked cakes and sent a parcel to France twice a week. That was the only thing she did into which she put all her energy. She disapproved when she saw her husband putting cigarettes into the parcel, and he also so much against them. The neighbours did the same.

"Since you are sending a parcel, put these cigarettes in for Twm," they would say. They said this, until their own sons went to the war.

There was no work to be had now in Moel Arian. The young and middle-aged had gone either into the army or into ammunition factories, or else to work in the docks in Liverpool and other places.

Now and again Ifan would go to unload ships in Holyhead, and then he would come back to work a bit on the farm. Whenever he worked on the docks, he was able to return home for the Sunday. It was a blessing that they had Eric now.

Those people who were at home began to ask themselves and others what was the meaning of it all. They had seen bad times very often. They had endured wrongs and injustices in the quarries; the tyranny of masters and owners, the oppression of favouritism and corruption. They had seen their friends and sons killed alongside them at work, but they had never experienced their children being taken away from them to be killed in war. Trying to find some explanation for it all, they discussed it from every angle in the Sunday School, for there was no quarry hut now in which they could talk things over.

They did not believe at all now that the war was being fought to save the smaller nations, or that it was a war to end all wars; neither did they believe that one nation was to blame more than another. They came to realise that in every country, there were people who regarded war as a good thing, and were taking advantage of their sons to promote their own interests. These were 'the Ruling Class', the same who oppressed them in the quarry, who sucked their blood and turned it into gold for themselves. Deep down, they believed by this time that some people were making money out of the war just as they had made money out of the bodies of the men in the quarries, and these were the people who wished to prolong the war. But they knew that if their sons refused to go, these people would be sure to come for them and take them by force.

The great problem for them in Sunday School was why God did not intervene, if God existed. Why did he always allow the poor to suffer? Just as there were great changes taking place in the world outside, their views began to change. Their faith in preachers and politicians was shaken. Preachers, who a short time before had been like little gods to them, were now condemned because they were in favour of the war. Some people stayed away from chapel for months because a preacher had spoken of the justice of the war. Similarly other preachers were idolised because they had declaimed against the injustice of it all. The people were unanimous in this; and the names of some famous politicians stank in their nostrils.

But the war continued. Many more of the boys came home in uniform, and the news of the deaths of some began to filter through.

In Tre Ffrwd, the same anxiety oppressed Owen. The same things went through his mind. He deplored the empty foolish talk that went on everywhere, and that from people generally considered intelligent. In that small town, there were people who spoke of the glory of war and the bravery of the boys, and they believed the newspapers word for word. It is true they worked hard to send comforts to the troops and to give them a welcome when they came home on leave, and so on, but their silly, empty talk and their cliche-ridden opinions, endlessly repeated, were enough to drive a person wild. Their sons would come home from the camps, and if they were officers, they would turn up their noses at people like Owen who dared to walk the streets in civilian clothes. Owen thought it was all very well for these boys, boys from the grammar school, who had been brought up in luxury and had never known what it was to go without anything; if they were suffering hardship now, it was for the first time. As for his own people, they had endured hardships all their lives, and as if that had not been enough, suddenly the war came like an invisible hand to crush them into the ground. He would like to go up to these erect, well-bred officers and tell them so. How were they, in the midst of their plenty, with their rich lowland pastures, to know or care about a little place like Moel Arian, with its thin crust of soil too poor to support such cattle as theirs? What could they know of the struggle to survive, wrenching a hard living from peat and clay? But sometimes that kind of land did produce some brains.

Some of the mistresses in the school began to reproach him for not enlisting. He sometimes felt like telling them that his call-up had been temporarily postponed because of his health, but he felt too ashamed. The only thing that would make him join was a feeling of loyalty to those of his friends and relatives who had already enlisted. He felt like this: if they were suffering, he should be with them, not because he agreed with the war, but because he sympathised with them. This came to trouble him more and more as letters arrived from Twm; not that his brother was complaining. The absence of complaints, when he knew there was so much to complain about, was what made him feel that he should go and suffer with Twm. But then he would think of them at home. He well knew what they were feeling now, and what they would feel if he were to enlist. But the next moment he felt a responsibility to be with Twm.

At school there was a young teacher named Ann Elis – a girl from Merionethshire. Owen had not spoken more than an occasional 'Good Morning' to her. She was strangely quiet, and some days would look very sad.

One day a telegram arrived for her to say that her young man had been killed in the trenches. When she returned to school a few days later, she seemed like one who had been grieving for months. Owen would have liked to go to her and tell her how sorry he was, but she now passed by him, and everybody else, without saying a word.

Within a month a telegram came for Owen asking him to come home, and nobody had to tell him what was the reason.

That morning, at the beginning of July, 1916, Jane Gruffydd was expecting a letter from Twm. She had not received one for six days. She was worried, but not too much because once before there had been a delay and then two letters arrived together. These days she could manage to do nothing but milk the cows and see Eric off to school before the postman came, and sometimes he would be late. He was late today, or he had already gone past. Yet she remained in her chair instead of going about her work. No, there was his whistle by the yard gate, and she ran out excitedly. But it was not a letter from Twm, nor was it from any of the other children. It was a long envelope with an official stamp on it. "Drat it," she said to herself, "another old form with questions to answer. They must think we own a thousand acre farm."

But when she opened it, she saw that it was not one of the usual forms. These were sheets of paper, written in English. She saw Twm's name, and his army number, and there was another sheet of thick white paper with only a few words on it in English.

She ran with the letter to the shop.

"Some old letter in English has come here, Richard Hughes. Will you tell me what it is? Something to do with Twm, anyhow."

The shopkeeper read it, and held it in his hand for a while.

"Sit down, Jane Gruffydd," he said gently.

"What is it?" she said. "Has anything happened?"

"Yes, I'm afraid so," he replied.

"Is he alive?"

"No, I'm afraid not."

He called from the shop to the kitchen, "Ann, please bring a glass of water."

Ann came through and held her arm, "Come through into the kitchen, Jane Gruffydd."

Later, she was taken back to Ffridd Felen.

Ifan was working for a few days at the hay harvest on a nearby farm, where the harvesting started earlier than at home.

When he saw a man crossing the field towards him, he knew why he was being called home.

All the children came home before nightfall. The neighbours came; they did the housework. They showed every kindness. And that night, after shutting the door behind the last of them, the children and their parents drew round the fire, for they felt that that was the way to be now that the first gap had been made in the family circle.

As Jane Gruffydd put her head down on the pillow and tried to close her eyes against the hurt, tens of sad thoughts came into her head. Amongst them was one further thought; she would not dread the sound of the postman again.

CHAPTER TWENTY-FOUR

In the world outside, there were great and sudden changes, but time stood still in Ffridd Felen. It was the same for every family in such circumstances but no one here knew or cared about any sadness but his own. There was no tomorrow. There remained only yesterday. The boys enlisted, news came of their deaths, and a hymn was sung to them in chapel; and although each family sympathised with other families, each person came back to his hearth with his own sadness.

The children became used to the aeroplanes which flew from the nearby mountain.

The time came for haymaking, a happy and festive time usually, when there was good weather; a time for enjoyment and fun; and for children, a time of good food with plenty of noise. But there was nothing of that in Ffridd Felen this year. They were girls, mostly, in the hayfields; they pitched the hay and made the loads. Wiliam did not come this year for he had only recently been there.

Owen had arrived home before the haymaking began. He worked top of the wagon or in the haystack. He tried to pretend that nothing had happened. Everybody else did the same. Nobody mentioned the cause of his grief. And yet there was only one thing at the back of everybody's mind.

Time dragged on; the Christmas holidays came and went, and oh! how everybody longed for them to go.

Before Owen came home the following summer, John Twnt i'r Mynydd had been killed, and one of the most difficult tasks that Owen had ever been required to do was to visit the family. He remembered the cheerfulness that had always been in Twnt i'r Mynydd. It was a house that seemed full of furniture, crockery and children, and as usual in such a house there was room for somebody else's chidren as well without anyone feeling they were in the way. Ann Ifans had changed so much that Owen felt for the first time in his life that there was no welcome for him there. But he tried to put himself in her place; a woman whose whole life seemed filled with laughter, never mind how low the wages were, or the price of animals. She was a woman who never let things like that trouble her. And now, when her comfort was taken away – that which had made her life so happy in the past – small wonder that she sank under her burden of grief. That was the way Ann Ifans had lived, clean and careful, always paying her way, but never making the carefulness a burden. She was wise enough to know that it would not pay her to be too ambitious for her children, never mind what other people's children did, but she wholeheartedly enjoyed herself in her husband's and children's company. They were allowed to play anywhere in the house and cowsheds, they could borrow ropes to make swings, they could climb trees, they could carry things from the house to make a den; and not only that, she would help them make the den herself, she would have the first go on the swing, and cover-up the damage done to the ropes. It would have been very difficult for Ann Ifans ever to discipline her children, but somehow the need never arose.

As Owen was leaving, she said to him, "It was you who used to walk with John to school long ago, wasn't it?"

"Yes," he said, and could think of nothing else to say.

"Come here again, Owen," she said, "come often, I shall be glad to see you."

And every time he went there afterwards, she would talk about John, and it was always on the same theme.

"You see, Owen, his employer was a thoroughly nasty and misely old man. He would have got blood from a stone if he had been able to."

"The headmaster in Twm's school was a nasty old man too."

"Heavens above, I thought Twm was in a good place."

"No, the head was a strict disciplinarian, half-killing the children and he would have killed his teachers too if he could."

"The poor, innocent creatures," she said.

Sometimes people would ask him to write letters for them to their sons in the army. It was not a difficult task when he was fairly familiar with the boys, but if they were much younger and he had forgotten them, it was very difficult indeed.

"What do you wish to tell Huw, John Jones?"

"Oh, you say what you think is best."

"Well, yes, I'll give them some of the news of the district, but what do you yourself want to say to Huw?"

"Tell him that his mother and I miss him very much, and hope he's safe and will soon be home again."

And that was all. They could never break out and disclose their innermost thoughts.

The holidays went by slowly. There was not much to do. The weather was wet. Dark clouds hung over Anglesey every day. The fields were green and the aftermath was thick. The purple of the heather and the yellow of the gorse were darkened and the crags on the mountainsides looked dark and forbidding. No sun came to strike the rocks or shrivel the heather. Yet it was difficult to churn, and the butter came out soft. His mother carried on with her usual work. She rarely spoke about Twm and did not show what she was feeling but Owen could tell from her manner that she was thinking of nothing but Twm. Sometimes she would say out of the blue, "Do you think it would have been better if Twm had gone back to College instead of taking that post in Llan Ddol?"

"No, I don't; I think he would have gone into the army sooner then."

"But then he might not have been killed."

And he knew she frequently dusted his brother's books in the best kitchen, although he never caught her at it.

He also came to realise that the fact that he was at home

was a great comfort to her. She did not show it, but her whole attitude seemed to change as the time to return to school neared. She prepared the food as usual. She boiled a lamb's head with the liver and chopped it into small pieces in the broth.

She pickled some herrings in August, and they all had to acknowledge that they enjoyed their food.

Eric was now ten years old and quite a sensible young lad. He had cried with the rest of the family when the news came about his uncle Twm, but he had then come to realise that any mention of him would give his grandmother pain; that is, talking about him in the way a child talks.

Owen was sorry for Eric. It was not much of a life for him, alone at Ffridd Felen, even though he was able to have many friends playing there. Now the summer holidays had come and there wasn't anywhere for him to go; just trotting round in his big, dusty boots all day. And yet, Owen supposed, it had been the same when they were children.

"I'm going to take Eric somewhere," he told his mother one fine day, which came between wet days. "You come, too, and perhaps we'll be able to persuade father."

"No, I shan't come," said his mother, as if she dreaded someone wanting her to go anywhere, "but Eric will be pleased. The lad hasn't had the chance to go anywhere much."

In Llandudno the two sat on the beach all afternoon, Eric paddling in the water and in perfect bliss.

"We'd better go and have some tea now, old man," said Owen. "What would you like?"

"Ice cream and cakes."

"Right then. Come on."

On the street, Owen saw a motor car pull up opposite the cafe he was going to. A soldier – an officer – got out of it followed by his sister, Sioned.

Owen grabbed hold of Eric and swung him round to face the other way.

"What's the matter, Uncle Owen?"

"I've suddenly remembered that there's an excellent place for ice cream in this street here."

"Better than that place?"

"Yes, much better."

Later, over tea, Eric said, "What's the matter, Uncle Owen? Don't you like the cake?"

"Yes, but it's giving me toothache."

"Try that one," said Eric. "There's no sugar in it."

Owen was reflecting on what he had seen. Once before, walking through the town, Owen had seen his sister in the company of some soldier. She was very beautiful this afternoon. She wore a black and white suit with a black hat, and did not look much older than when she was married.

"Lucky the child did not see her," he said to himself, "and I'll have to hold my tongue about it when I get home."

"Now then, Eric, what else for you?"

"Nothing, thanks. I've stuffed myself full."

"Well, we'll go and have a little look around the shops now, and see the little birds."

"We must buy something for Grandma and Grandad, mustn't we, Uncle Owen?"

"Yes, indeed; lucky you remembered."

"I've been thinking about it all morning, and I'd like to buy something for Llew, too."

"Who's Llew?"

"You know, that little boy who lives in Jane Williams' house. She's his grandma."

"Right, we'll go then."

When they were sitting on the sand once more, with a pipe for Grandad, and a little jug for Grandma, and a fishing net for Llew in their pockets, Owen asked, "What would you like to do when you grow up, Eric?"

"Be a printer, the same as Wmffra, Bryn Arian."

"Wouldn't you like to carry on in school?"

"No; I prefer to mess around with engines and things like that."

"How do you know you'd like to be a printer?"

"Well, one day, Aunty Bet and I went to see the place were Wmffra is working, and Wmffra says that I can go there as an apprentice. But remember, I'll be coming home to sleep with Grandma and Grandad and not at my Mother's."

"Oh, it's too soon to decide things like that."

The fine weather came in September, when it was almost time for Owen to return to school, and he did not relish the idea at all. Some mornings he used to go out picking blackberries for his mother to make jam.

The last Monday of his holidays, he got up at about six o'clock and went to pick some in Ceunant Woods. In the silence of the woods he suffered one of those fits of depression which came after the death of his brother. It was so quiet that even the gentle sound of the brook was magnified. When something rustled in the undergrowth, a cold shiver went through him. The haze slowly rose from the face of the sea and the heat of the sun increased. The fields were drenched with dew. Traces of where the cows had been lying before they were called to milking could be seen standing out lighter against the surrounding grass. As he sat on a stone, he could almost feel the heat of the cow where she had lain. He remembered all those times he had been blackberrying with his brother, usually after school, and he could now almost recapture the scent of trees in the clear light of a September evening, and they with their pockets bulging with nuts. The night would quickly gather round them and they would run home, their brows dripping with sweat. Their mother would be glad of the blackberries. He remembered how Twm would expect his mother to make a pudding that very night, but he would fall asleep before undressing. He remembered how they would enjoy the pudding the next evening, and then go out to sit on the wall, cracking nuts, exactly as Eric did nowadays. How warm and dark the kitchen had been, and how delightful it was to sit on the broad plank of the stile across the wall just outside.

But what was the use of dreaming? These things belonged to another life. It seemed almost as if it had happened to another person. He felt hungry. He knew that despite his sadness, it was his parents who had been struck the cruellest blow.

But recently, when he had been depressed like this, a ray of hope had come to him. His school life was not as monotonous as it used to be. So far Ann Elis and himself were the only two to have lost somebody in the war. That grew into a bond of friendship between them for they were now able to talk together and about something which they could not discuss with anybody else. They talked endlessly about the injustice of everything, and above all about the inability of people to see things correctly. They always felt better after having a chat like that. It was this that gave Owen the hope that he might be able to live fully, despite his loss.

When he arrived home, there was a stranger present. He was a military pensions officer. A short time before, Owen had requested a pension for his mother, on the grounds that apprentices killed in the war received a compensation, paid to the parents. The officer had long complicated forms which needed filling-out. What was Twm's salary for the year he taught? What did his father earn, and what did the other children earn? How much money did they have at Ffridd Felen?

He shook his head dubiously, as if to imply that there was too much money coming in.

Jane Gruffydd said, "You'd better not think that I get anything from any of the children except from that one," pointing at Owen, "and really, he shouldn't be giving anything either, because his salary has not kept up with the cost of living. My husband only works sometimes. And if the price of butter and pigs has gone up, so too have feeding costs, and the rate of interest on the money we've had to borrow has gone up as well."

"But the other children can help you."

"No, indeed, they can't. The wages of two of the girls have gone up very little, and the boy has a family of his own."

"Well, I'll see what I can do," he said, placing the papers in his pocket, "though I'm promising nothing."

He looked self-satisfied and well-fed.

"What's the name of that widow who lives up here?" he asked. "She lost a son in the war."

"Oh, Margiad Owen, Coedfryn."

"Yes, that's it. I had to reduce her pension this week."

Owen and his mother looked at him, astonished, for they knew Margiad Owen's circumstances well enough to know that twelve shillings a week was not half enough for her to live on.

"I reduced it from twelve shillings a week to eight shillings because she keeps hens and makes a bit of money selling eggs."

At that moment a strange feeling came over Jane Gruffydd. For fifteen long months, a deep resentment had been gathering in her very soul against everything that was responsible for the war, against man and against God. And when she saw this plump man in his immaculate clothes preening himself on the fact that he had reduced a widow's pension, she lost control of herself. It was like a dam bursting. At that noment, the man standing before her represented all that was behind the War. She grabbed the nearest thing to hand – a clothes-brush – and struck him on the head with it.

"Get out of this house at once," she shouted.

The man was glad to make his escape.

"My dear son," she cried out. "And something like you is allowed to live."

Both she and Owen broke down and wept.

CHAPTER TWENTY-FIVE

That same night, Owen was sitting in the kitchen after his mother and father had gone to bed. He could not think of sleep because of the deep disturbance in his mind. It was almost like the day when the news came that Twm had been killed. He and his mother had allowed their feelings to flood over them. And yet he did not feel better for it. Instead of being concentrated on his brother, his thoughts now ran in all directions. The pensions officer had thrown a stone into the middle of a pond and Owen could not tell where the commotion would end. Before this, his brother's death had filled the compass of his thoughts and feelings. It was as if the War had singled out their family and struck down Twm in revenge on them all.

From now on his brother's death would lie hard and cold on his heart, but his mind would work in other directions. Until now the war had affected him only passively. He had endured it with fear and hope as some inevitable fate that had fallen on the world, fearing that the worst would happen to his family and desperately hoping that it would not. In the midst of it all he had seen a lot of kindness mixed-up with foolish, silly talk. He had heard of War profiteers; he had even seen them from a distance. But today he had come face-to-face with a cruel action performed by one of his own people, as it were. Strangely enough, it was not that he was afraid of his mother being taken to court for hitting the man, neither was he worried lest she not receive the pension, but it was the cruelty of the whole thing that hurt him deeply. That was how it was in war; it was not only the killing and the suffering that was cruel, but also incidents like this. And there was his mother having to have somebody to translate into Welsh the news that her son had been killed!

The thought of it made him sweat, and the kitchen became insufferable. He turned down the lamp and went out in the direction of the mountain. It was a clear moonlit night and the path was a greyish white underfoot. Now and again a sheep rose from its resting place, disturbed by the sound of his tread, and ran somewhere else. The streams flowed so quietly; it was as if they were just swirling around and not scudding along. He sat down on a big stone. The village lay beneath him like a fairyland under the spell of the moon. Here and there, like dark smudges, were the little farmhouses and their yards, sheltered by their clumps of trees. The moon shone on the houses, the light reflected from their slate roofs. The houses cast long shadows before them, and the fields looked strangely yellow in that light. In the bottom field of all the corn stood in stooks. Around him, where he sat, the land was reddish black and Owen knew that all land, as far as the eye could see, had been like that once – about a hundred years before. Those who had toiled to turn that barren land into green pastures were by now lying in the parish cemetery in that more fertile soil that lay between him and the sea. Some of them had come from the bottom of the valley to cultivate the high mountain land and to rear their families, and then returned to their original environment for their 'long sleep'.

And yet the real handiwork of those toil-worn hands was not visible to him. In his mind's eye, he could visualise many countries all over the world, where there were great cities with countless streets, and they had Moel Arian slates on their roofs. And the same moon which shone on the houses in Moel Arian tonight would be casting its beams to slide over the roofs of those houses in distant lands.

He turned his eyes towards the quarry tip. Tonight it was but a black patch on the mountainside. Those same people who had wrested the small farms from the mountain peatlands had been responsible for the quarry tip too. Between these two, for a hundred years, the villagers had worked from dawn to dusk making their backs bend before they reached middle-age. Some of them had hoped that, by sending their children to schools, to offices, shops, they would escape from it all.

His thoughts came back to his own family. They were typical of the families of the district, a hard-working people who'd had their share of trouble, trying to pay their way and frequently failing, and then when there was an end to debt in sight and the prospect of an easier life for his parents, here was a cruel unexpected blow.

He remembered Ann Ifans once saying what grand clothes his mother had when she first came to the district. She never had new clothes now. She had some after Twm's death but had never worn them again. He remembered how well she looked on that prize-giving day at the County School. He was the only one who had tried to make things easier for his parents, although he was not the only one capable of doing so. He did not consider that a virtue – he was soft, that was all. He could not help it. In a way, it was his selfishness. He had felt strongly attracted to his mother since he was small; he wanted all her care for himself, but he never got it. He had her generosity and her care, but not her love. He wondered if the other children had felt the same. Apart from Elin, home was nothing to the others. Sometimes Owen suspected that Twm had been nearer to his mother's heart than all the other children, but he had no proof of that. Probably she would have felt the same if she had lost him – Owen – in the war.

His parents had never been ones to show their emotions, and it was difficult to know what really gave them pleasure. They enjoyed many things, but he knew for certain that what they looked forward to most of all was to be free from debt and to enjoy a retirement without worry at the end of their lives. In this way they were not very different from the rest of mankind. That was why Owen thought this calamity was such a grievous one for them. When freedom from debt was in sight, they were struck down by this unexpected blow.

That was what always drew him towards his mother and made him try to forget Ann Elis. Ever since his foolish love-affair with Gwen long ago, no girl had appealed to him as much as Ann. He had not yet fallen in love with her, but he liked her very much. At school, all day long he looked forward to the evening when he would have a chat with her. In today's fit of depression when he had been blackberrying, thinking about her had given him the only ray of hope that he would ever feel better. But now the incident of the pensions officer had changed things again. It was not the financial side that affected him, but the emotional. He was once again drawn closer to his mother.

And his eyes were opened to the possibility of doing something instead of simply enduring like a dumb animal. It was about time that somebody challenged this injustice and did something about it. Come to think of it, that was what was wrong with his people. They were courageous in their capacity to endure pain, but would do nothing to get rid of what caused that pain. Wiliam was the only member of the family who had stood out against things as they were, unless you could say that Sioned had done so. Perhaps she was showing her antipathy towards the way his family lived, by living her own life according to completely different stan-dards. Twm had turned his back on the home and had shown that he was capable of leaving it. He, Owen, was a coward, that was the truth of it. He had let his mother hit that pensions officer this morning, instead of hitting him himself. He had never left home, to go to school or college, without feeling homesick to the point of vomiting.

He looked around him at the countryside. Were it not for the dimmed lights of the town, nobody could say there was a war on. It was difficult to believe that a little out-of-the-way corner of Wales had a part to play in the War. And yet the vile tentacles of that monster reached into the deepest recesses of the mountains. A few weeks ago, a local boy had deserted from the army and had hidden for a week in a cave, going home to have supper with his mother every night. But the army bloodhounds had discovered him, and he was seen being led to the railway station looking like one defeated. Within three days news came that he had been killed in France, and his family and most of the people in the locality were innocent enough to believe it. Why did they not rise up against such things? But what was he saying? He, himself, was one of them. Sometimes he thought it would have been better if his ancestors had stayed on the other side of the Eifl mountains in Lleyn and just tilled the soil.

But perhaps, after all, he expected too rounded and complete a pattern of life, taking it for granted that things would turn out all right if only he did his duty. But there was no hope of knitting-up the ravelled threads of people's lives.

He got up from the stone and saw that there was something familiar about it. Examining it closely, he saw that a number of names had been scratched upon it, his own amongst them. Four of them had been killed in the War. T.G. was there, clearly to be seen, cut more recently than O.G. He remembered that when they used to fetch heather to light the fire in the morning this was the stone on which they had rested their loads before humping them higher on their backs and setting off on the track down the mountain. Walking down the same way now, the smell of heather and peat came to him again – the heather scratching his neck and the peat trickling down between his shirt and skin so that it seemed to him like thousands of ants.

When he arrived home, the cat was sitting on the door-step. It rubbed itself fondly against his legs and followed him into the house with its tail high in the air. He turned up the

flame in the lamp and gave the fire a poke. The cat continued to press itself against his legs purring contentedly. He sat down in the armchair and reached for his pipe to have a smoke, the first that day.

THE AUTHOR

Kate Roberts was born in 1891 in Rhosgadfan near Caernarfon, in Wales' slate-quarrying heartland. Widely regarded as the twentieth century's outstanding Welsh-language novelist, she defined Welsh fiction for decades, and as publisher, critic and political activist had a huge influence on Welsh culture. She died in 1985.

Also by Kate Roberts and available from Seren:
Tea in the Heather (Te yn y Grug)
Translated by Wyn Griffith